THE BIG ROOM

Guy Peellaert   Michael Herr

Summit Books · New York

For Peter, with special thanks to Elisabeth Peellaert and Anne Herouet. –G.P.

For Sonny Mehta. –M.H.

Copyright © 1986 by Guy Peellaert and Michael Herr
All rights reserved
including the right of reproduction in whole or in part
in any form
Published by SUMMIT BOOKS
A Division of Simon & Schuster, Inc.
Simon & Schuster Building, 1230 Avenue of the Americas
New York, New York 10020
Published by arrangement with
Verlag Walther H. Schünemann GmbH & Co., Munich
SUMMIT BOOKS and colophon are trademarks
of Simon & Schuster, Inc.

Designed by Hans Peter Weiss and René Walker

Manufactured in West Germany
1 2 3 4 5 6 7 8 9 10

Library of Congress Cataloging-in-Publication-Data

Peellaert, Guy.
    The big room.

    1. Las Vegas (Nev.)–Popular culture–History–20th century.
    2. Celebrities–Nevada–Las Vegas.   3. United States–Popular culture–History–20th century.
I. Herr, Michael.   II. Title.
F849.L35P44   1986   979.3'13   86-5811
ISBN 0-671-63028-8

CONTENTS

The transient attractions of the Museum were constantly diversified, and educated dogs, industrious fleas, automatons, jugglers, ventriloquists, living statues, tableaux, gipsies, Albinos, fat boys, giants, dwarfs, rope-dancers, live "Yankees", pantomime, instrumental music, singing and dancing in great variety, dioramas, panoramas... mechanical figures... dissolving views... these, among others, were all exceedingly successful.

—Barnum, *Struggles and Triumphs*

I

The desert here was always a closed system. Not the lowest nor the hottest, less than forbidding but more than uninviting, it was a stretch of the West that struck everyone who saw it in the early days as mean, eco-exclusive, just not too attractive.

In 1844, when Frémont and his troop passed through on their way to California, and there were still traces over the ground of the meadows for which it was named, it wasn't thought to be good for anything more than a fast bivouac. Frémont was the great advance man for the opening of the West, exploring possibilities more than land routes, anticipating (therefore finding) prodigies of beauty and opportunity around every bend in the trail, raving and tummeling all the way to the Coast, while his cartographer, a European named Charles Preuss, saw almost nothing but ominous alien emptiness. They rode side by side and kept their journals, and while none of their physical boundaries have held, the descriptive boundaries they made together are still true, mapping the extremes of westering mind: smash-flop, boom-bust, heaven-hell. Passing through Nevada, discoverers at this stage of practically nothing, they were a couple of well-connected heavily funded drifters at the head of an army of drifters, opening a route for the generations of drifters to come. It's not likely, when the expedition finally reached California, that any of its members even remembered this spot, or looked out over the Pacific at sundown and reminisced, *Las Vegas, fabulous place*.

Those were the days of frontier as frontier, with miles of unknown, unsettled land left to support the innocent connections between "Frontier" and "Geography". Territorial perfection: As long as Manifest Destiny was the national obsession, the continental Edge was the biggest attraction. When the 49ers came through, going for the gold, they were going for the rest of the package too; the big sky and the sweetwater, the infinities of vertical space; and for the kicks. Moving slower than hard time through brittle-bush, ocotillo, yucca, monkey flower, sage, salt-brush, columbine and creosote, heading for real and presumed goldstreams along the coast, they made camp here. Singing and dancing and telling stories, praying all night for strength, safety and a huge return on their tremendous investment, a-sleep and dreaming about the pay-off or lying awake whispering and sighing, they formed the pioneer projection, and filled the thin skies over Las Vegas with the propaganda of plenty. And in the morning moved on.

Of course, in order to get across that terrain, they could never really let themselves believe that the line might read "California *and* Bust". Yet for every pilgrim who found enduring wealth, there were tens of thousands who lost everything. Shooting the azimuth with their bodies, sweating and straining (and let's not forget

dying) against the obvious north-south geo-physical American grain, they came up empty. Their disappointment can not only be imagined, it can still be felt today, the historical corollary to the tall tale about the survivors of the journey who found rest at last in California, setting themselves energetically to civilization-making. More likely, almost everyone who got across the deserts and plains came out of it tired and haunted and so phobic that they couldn't get any rest from their sleep ever again unless there was something in their line of vision that was bigger than they were, and man-made.

Las Vegas lay there baking in the sun for another hundred years. The alkali got the meadow, making it even more useless than before. The Army couldn't use it. The Mormons who came down to extend their Utah empire couldn't use it. And the native Paiute who helped drive the Mormons away, more by their pesky shiftless intransigence than by any violence, didn't seem to have much use for it either. (Besides which, in their brutish heathen "religion", ostentation was considered not only blasphemous, but impractical.) The great Nevada gold and silver strikes came into the north, Comstock and Ophir making towns that grew up, flourished and disappeared in a few years' time, while Vegas stayed level with the desert. The railroad put down a division point on its California line there, but hardly anyone got off. As late as the day of its incorporation in 1905, it was just a tent town, even its big hotel was made of canvas; and no one there still with any idea of what it would become, or what used for.

Until it was clear to everyone that all the frontier that there was ever going to be had been completely used up, every land limit reached and all the ground consumed, while frontier hunger continued unappeased, and when they couldn't take it any farther out on American soil, they brought it back in again to Las Vegas, and did it farther out that way. In this scrubby, nowhere place, so totally and profoundly Nowhere that it stood as motionless and confusing as a mirror. A mirror and a mirage where the great lines of a great nation converged in the physical representation of mental American infinity and made their great run out towards vanishing point.

Parentheses: History Takes a Holiday

Lost Wages: Not for the finicky rabid law of the settled west, but its suspension. Not for roots but for their guaranteed absence, to institutionalize drift as a right and a principal. Not a fit place for women and children, or children anyway, but for adult rush and release, for fun. Socked in there so perfectly between Death Valley and Paradise Valley, John Milton couldn't have put it any closer to the dime. As the Preacher said to the Whore, the Lord must write his own stuff, because that's a terrific gag, and the history routine is even better:

October, 1849: Kit Carson, in wild pursuit of a raiding party of the Jacarilla Apache, overrides their camp and finds, among the baggage stolen from a wagon train, a book published in New York about himself and his exploits, a work of unauthorized highly romantic heroic fiction which the one man who should have known better apparently took so seriously that he was never the same old Kit again. There he was, just living his glorious (according to Frémont, his greatest fan) and/or vicious (according to Preuss, still on the expedition but never with the program) life, and he found himself caught, lifted instantly into legend and celebrity. This is probably the first instance in America of spontaneous star psychosis, or a star recognizing himself all of a sudden as a star in public.

Meanwhile (easily the most poignant word in the historian's grammar): Same year, same month, probably same hour: P. T. Barnum opens negotiations which bring Jenny Lind to the United States to play what will one day be known as the big room and creating, if not the room itself, a need for the room and a deep insatiable national longing for it, by booking an attraction that would have filled such a room many times over. And with a class act too, not the fakes and freaks upon which his great fortune and all of American show business were founded. ("My organ of 'acquisitiveness' was manifest at an early age," he wrote in his memoirs. "When I was six years old my capital amounted to a sum sufficient to exchange for a silver dollar. Nor did my dollar long remain alone.")

Of course history is formed out of the same artificial categories as culture, high and low, and you have to watch the parentheses like a hawk. Time and the big events settle officially into the past, they compact and shift like plates in the earth until one day a little piece snaps off from the footnotes and shoots up to the historian's brain, a data embolism, and he can't see the text any more for the subtext. It's possible that Carson and Barnum may have met, but it's obvious to all of us today, with what we know, that they were on the same circuit, connecting Broadway to Sutter's Mill, and understanding that it was a necessary connection, and definitely historical. Because a big country needs a big room (Barnum), and a big room needs a big country (Carson).

Just as you didn't have to be a farmer in those days to believe that rain follows the plow, Carson demonstrated that you didn't have to be in the theatre to have a great act. As for Barnum, what can you say? The man belongs on Mt. Rushmore. His seed may have been the most powerful of all, stronger than Jefferson's or Paine's, Lincoln's or even Poe's. It grew a show business heaven on American earth, a *matto grosso el dorado* of entertainment. Today there's no citizen too poor, sick, hungry or disenfranchised to be deprived of his portion day or night, in peace or wartime. There's no business not like show business, all along the sliding curve. Not too many of Barnum's beneficiaries still think they're living in the cradle of the millenium, or nourish the dream of the mystical Union, or any Union at all, but we all know how we feel about image. Everybody wants the big room, and they say that if you really want it badly enough, you can have it.

II

All the passions produce prodigies. A gambler is capable of watching and fasting, almost like a saint . . .

— Simone Weil

Crazy little place, Las Vegas, really wild, totally fabulous, fantastic. If you go you'll have a fabulous time, and if you never make it there you might spend the rest of your life thinking what you've missed, imagining that it's not just totally but literally fabulous, like the Fox and the Crow, or the Belly and the Other Members; and clinically fantastic, the picture card hidden up Scheherezaade's sleeves for a thousand nights in case she has to play it before the last morning, and if that doesn't get it she'll fold like a lady, cut off her own head, and leave it on the table for the house. That kind of thing goes on in Vegas all the time.

And can one of you good people please tell me, what are they talking about in New York and L.A., what do they mean, "too Las Vegas"? The word "excess" doesn't even apply here. It's just another lost empty thought-form blowing down the Strip and out of town on the Washoe Zephyr to make room for new faces and fresher blood, no reference anywhere to validate it in a city whose scale was never really determined, locked, confined by ceiling. You could be prissy and say that that's because greed has no ceiling, and that the whole scam was gotten up in the first place behind the single, base hunch that inside every straight citizen lay a degenerate gambler, a lush and a whorehound, or that with or without ceiling, it's nothing but a low vulgar place. But it was prissiness of a kind that almost ruined Las Vegas, in the Howard Hughes years, when all the big hotels were crawling with retired FBIs and corporate-Mormon regulators, all so besotted with bottom-line mind that they couldn't see how the action was shaped. (For not only had the Army returned to Las Vegas, and half of California; Lo, even the Mormons returned, although almost everything that went on there was strictly proscribed by the Angel Moroni; and with stunning resourcefulness found the means to participate in the take without iniquitous trespass, the type of behaviour commemorated in the old expression, "As accommodating as a Mormon.")

Some say that Hughes' Las Vegas tenure ended because he lost interest in it, his whim taking flight from repeated shocks caused by the nuclear tests a hundred miles to the north that have always been such a feature of Las Vegas life. (He offered to pay the government to conduct the tests someplace else, anyplace else, but the government wasn't interested in his money in that form, and he grew tired of spending so much time under his bed.) It's more likely that Hughes' organizational style was simply rejected by Las Vegas, like a toxin. It was making the regulars nervous, and it mitigated against impulse, the founding principal. It was attempting to upgrade a reputation whose only value in the first place lay in offering everybody the same shot at the kind of life that Hughes had always enjoyed, or not enjoyed, but anyway lived. Even very rich losers are not as popular in Las Vegas as is usually supposed. There's always the Bringdown Factor: Who cares that you're rich if you're not having any fun?

◆

Soft desert night, flash marquee, stone foxes shake their boxes and everybody's a winner, potentially. Las Vegas loves lovers, controlled love in a controlled environment, and it loves winners, up to a point. Real love and substantial winnings, at least as substantial as the neon, xenon, argon and krypton tracking through a hundred thousand miles of tubing: "Noble Gases", but finally only gases, vapours, with all the properties and habits of a phantom, overwhelmingly present prior to evaporation. Whoever imagined that light without heat could be so romantic, and so inspiring? When you're a hit, you see the lights when they're not even on, and when you bomb you barely notice them at all. It couldn't be any more real, or any more symbolic. Those people you hear about who came into town on a Greyhound and left a few hours later in a Ferrari may be anonymous, but they're not apocryphal. Ask them if Las Vegas is real. Ask them if it's symbolic.

Probably no place else in the history of modern city building was developed on a single idea the way Las Vegas was. The closest thing to it is Hollywood, which grew by exporting its idea, but the Vegas idea can't leave town. It has nothing for export but its promise. Its growth was not only conspicuous, conspicuousness was the only medium of its growth. You can't touch conspicuousness, it's like efflorescence. You can feel it and walk around in it and, when you're in Vegas, hold the more than reasonable hope that it will materialize for you; the Passion According to St. Nick the Greek. When the town finally raised itself up above the desert floor and began radiating and broadcasting itself, the rebounding waves drew millions in, and not just the loose pins and shavings of a restless moneymad tourist population, but Personalities, men and women of tremendous stature, and weight, and density. They pronounced it fabulous, and inimitable, and never

11

stopped to ask why it was, and has always been, that almost everybody who comes here for the first time has the feeling that they've been here before. And not just before, but all along.

Arriving off the long trail of a thousand cities and towns, one so much like the others as to be indistinguishable, into the packaged premeditated trumped up (true) West, Howdy do drop in, come as you are, do what you want, what you'd never dare to do back home, at least not openly, piss away the hours with the nickles and dimes or get in deep, too deep, even drown, if that's your pleasure. Roaring in from L.A. and New York, Dallas, Detroit, Miami, New Orleans (London, Paris, Tokyo, Caracas, Bahrain, New Delhi) engorged and dying to pop, driven over the earth by undifferentiated wants into the receptacle and outlet, material gulag and dream terminal, to breathe the air of license and "personal" freedom: a few laughs, a few drinks, company, and all of it legal, or most of it, a lot of it, sort of. Your money is as good as anybody else's money, and it doesn't come fairer than that, or more democratic. Protracted Helldorado, where the only inhibitor of your appetites is your means, and the only thing that isn't promiscuous is the percentage.

◆

When they talk about luck in Las Vegas, it's just the way they have there of talking about time. Luck is the local obsession, while time itself is a sore subject in the big rooms and casinos. It's a corny old gag about Las Vegas, the temporal city if there ever was one, trying to camouflage the hours and retard the dawn, when everybody knows that if you're feeling lucky you're really feeling time in its rawest form, and if you're not feeling lucky, they've got a clock at the bus station. For a speedy town like Vegas, having no time on the walls can only accelerate the process by which jellyfish turn into barracuda, grinders and dumpers become a single player, the big winners and big losers exchange wardrobes, while everyone gets ready for the next roll. The whole city's a clock. The hotels change credit lines as fast and often as they change the sheets, and for a lot of the same reasons. The winners and the losers all have identical marks on them, bruised and chewed over by Las Vegas mitosis, with consolation prizes for anybody left who's not already inconsolable. Don't laugh, people. It could happen to you.

III

They Smile When They Are Low . . .

You know them all, legends in their own time in their own space. You know them, and they can't quite place you. Sometimes, in our understandable hunger to be where we think they are, we form the crazy belief that we actually *know* them, but this isn't usually so. Mostly, they only know each other, bonded smoothly and exclusively through connections of interest and experience, billing and credentials, money, power and skin, and that leaves us out. No room could ever hold them all. We wouldn't know where to look, the focus would go, we'd cancel out each other's force, ruining whatever relationship we ever had, until we became attraction and they became audience. That's how delicate the balance is, and how intimate.

It's a very sentimental business, you've got to be tough. Every star has a secret or two about how they came up, but one thing is clear: We made them, and we can unmake them. If they avoid us, it might hurt our feelings, but if we avoid them, they're finished. And if we just gave it to everybody who wanted it, there'd be nobody left to work the lounges, to stand below the glamour-line and confront the overflows, while everything they ever wanted is going on for someone else upstairs. They make a good living, lounge acts, and live in hope, and are good troupers; that is, seasoned infantry shoring up the sagging line all along the entertainment front. They're talent too, but very few of us ever go all the way to Las Vegas to see them. We don't adore them. Sometimes we barely tolerate them. On a good night, when everything works and it feels so right, they might think they're ready for the big room, but the fact usually is that they're too ready, and we know it even if they don't. Onstage or off, it occurs to very few of us that we could be doing them a favor.

◆

It's hardly in anybody's nature to want less and less of a good thing. Very few people go into show business to mortify their own flesh. It's great when you're on top, or so they say, but when the stars go down they know a pain that lounge acts never know. We all can remember acts that used to pull fifty grand a week and more who can't get five now, and if they still had what they made, couldn't buy their way back inside for even one night: Athletes too old and slow, politicians found out in their grubby little grafts, baritones whose voices have grown cold and loveless, novelties who thought they were necessities, wise guys with their nuts caught in the power squeeze, all the public darlings of a few moments ago who are nobody's darlings now. Washed up, moving sometimes gracefully, always painfully, towards the elephant's graveyard of public affection, necro-nostalgia, and the old stale showbiz crapola. The gone-but-not-forgotten, and that's the worst part. They're not forgotten at all but recalled, and pitied. True, they're released from certain terrible pressures. They don't have to worry about career moves any more, and they'll always have their memories. When there's nothing left to cry about, they can always bring those up.

At some point in every great career, looking back becomes the same as looking down. Great burdens at great heights, a precariousness that not even the greatest stars can overcome. Their fame precedes them, but it follows them too, like a beast on a leash. It cushions and hides them and generally informs them in the day to day conduct of their careers, but there's a tax on every move they make. Our intrusions, when they're successful, are more against their isolation than their privacy. Inevitably, they become living breathing coming attractions for themselves. The shell between their outermost and their innermost is thinner but tougher than most people's, as anyone knows who ever got on an elevator with Frank Sinatra, or dreamed that they were making love to Marilyn Monroe.

Some have actually made it overnight, rockets who shot up so fast from the bottom that they couldn't pull loose in time and brought the bottom up with them. But most, nearly all, achieve it slowly, by whatever method, and that's

better. The big room is not a clearing that anyone should charge into blindly, unarmed. The way in is hard, as dangerous as the approach to King Solomon's Mines, and obscure as a tomb. In fact, many a headliner has had good reason to compare the room to the tomb, having experienced for themselves the non-contradiction that once you've made it here, it's all over for you.

Because the big room is a trick room. For a space that has always been imbued with such magic, it's remarkably neutral. It's as indifferent to great success as it is to ambition without talent. It's one of those star chambers, like Prospero's Cell, Faust's Study, or the Oval Office, charged with moral to say the least ambiguity, filled with action and thought, yet constant, mute and undynamic. Nobody has ever been hot enough to change its temperature a degree, or dent its integrity, its justice. It's where the high road was always going, and when you've finally played it, you see that you can only play it again. For more money maybe, or to larger, warmer audiences. You can go on carrying your crowds away with you on the buoyancy of your shameless inflations, or count on them to remember for you what you've forgotten, or lost interest in. A lot of names who meant only to settle into their act ended by hardening into it instead, but they were so big that nobody seemed to notice, or care. Many stars, realizing that they're in a museum, learn to play it with grace, making long and loving relationships with their fans. The best start playing to themselves again, as they did when they were first breaking in, going deeper and even deeper inside for their act, to move themselves, and to last. But beyond that, nothing. There is no other, bigger room.

When you consider that it had so much mystery about it going in, and was so hard to enter, the exits are incredibly, even blatantly, well marked. You wouldn't think that so many people could have so much trouble recognizing them. The spirits of the room aren't malicious, but they're far from benign. They would never intervene by taking a loser and making him look like a winner. (As any Las Vegas old-timer knows, a loser is just a player who hates to win.) It's really only physics, implacable showbiz physics, where the strongest light throws the coldest shadow. Sometimes the shadows take over and have long careers of their own. And sometimes a star cools so quickly that there's no time to slide. He's projected clean through the walls of the room, and when they go out like that they don't leave a vacuum in the room behind them, they take the vacuum with them. You should see the big room when it's empty. It looks even bigger.

◆

But this isn't showtime anymore. No matter what you've heard, nobody is really on all the time. Everybody needs a breather between shows, a moment alone to rest and unwind, to prepare for one of those second acts that aren't supposed to exist in American life.

The stage is empty but animated. While they're bussing up the tables we file out, flushed with other people's success. Back to the casinos and the action, back to our cars and the road, back to our rooms to lie quietly on the bed and make the Vegas meditation, the same one the stars make, Am I Up or Am I Down? Were we really as wonderful as they said we were? Out of the big room into the long room, the portrait gallery of our creation. Because let's face it ladies and gentlemen, even those of us who don't think of ourselves as being particularly creative made this one, we made it all together. It's as long as our memories, and if it seems to narrow and darken at the far end, that's just an illusion, as you'll see when you've walked it for yourself. There's nothing to be nervous about, we've been working together for years, we're terrific and we love each other very much. We'll be a wonderful audience, and they'll just be what they've always been. Let's really mean it then. Let's all go in. Let's all respond.

F.D.R. / BUGSY SIEGEL

There has never been another place like it for connecting the unconnectable, and if you doubt it look at this pair, dealt spontaneously from the great American deck. One off the top, a king with the value of four aces, and one from the bottom, the wildest card in the pack. The patrician, destiny's giant and history's client, in the books and on the dime, not just another president, and president of more than the United States, president by a landslide of the Twentieth Century itself. And this menace, this lowlife gutter-snake mobster, but not just another mobster; the outlaw *par excellence*, from his baby-blue eyes down to his alligator shoes, his Broadway/Hollywood pals, and his tender-hardboiled love story, co-starring Virginia Hill.

F.D.R. and Bugsy Siegel were far from bedfellows, but they weren't complete opposites either. Each had developed his patented blend of seductiveness and iron, each acquired a legendary stature (like Honest Abe and Billy the Kid, although the Bug probably killed a lot more people than the Kid), and each, in his time and in his way, was a traitor to his class. Roosevelt was the most uncontrollably democratic man that American privilege had ever produced, and Ben Siegel longed endlessly (well, extensively) for greater ex-

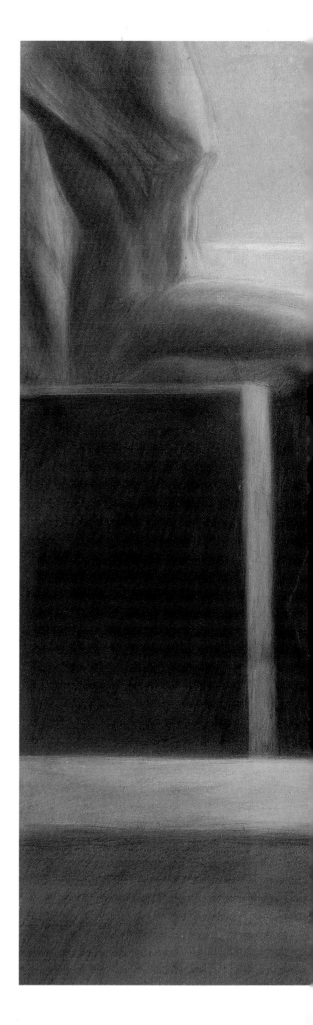

The Dam. 1984

The Flamingo. 1983

clusivity. Each man had his own idea of where the equalizer lay, and what steps he could take to arm and activate it. Maybe Las Vegas never had a mother, but it was rich in fathers, and these two, in dreams and in fact, were first among them.

◆

Franklin Roosevelt was the ceremonial father, presiding as he did at the opening of Hoover, née Boulder, Dam in September, 1935. When he threw the switch and the juice came down like paternal grace it ran straight to Las Vegas, twenty-five miles away, just as the dam builders themselves had been doing nights and weekends for the five years it took to complete the work, establishing the town's usage for all time.

Benjamin Siegel was the practical father, although his associates in the east didn't think he was being very practical at all, pouring their money like that into his outrageous plan. How those dark eyebrows went up when he told them it would take two million to build, and how they came down again when the cost eventually reached six million. In fact, from the day in 1945 when he first pulled off of Highway 91 and pointed towards the emptiness and said, decreed, fatally *insisted*, that right there in the middle of what looked just like nowhere to everyone else, he would build his fabulous Flamingo Hotel, they really wondered about him. And when he told them that once his movie-star and society friends from L.A. started the ball rolling, the rich, powerful and famous would come there from all over the world, and by a transfer of much more than their money would make the Flamingo rich powerful and famous (and the man behind it would rise up so classy and legitimate that his gruesome past would dissolve, except for the least controlled whisper, for glamour), they thought that he was madder than the maddest drifter in the desert, and, being Bugsy, a thousand times more dangerous.

◆

The dam had not been Roosevelt's idea, but he was quick and inspired to see what it was good for. First of the seven wonders of the modern world, it was the massive poured concrete substitute for the miracle Depression America needed, and fully expected; so tremendously potent and good-looking that many people accepted it for the miracle itself. It's strange to think how devotional they became about something as thick, hard and present as Boulder Dam. For F.D.R. it was the pumping, working symbol of a whole new deal: Power not only to the southwest, but to all the people; a great field of federal warmth; shelter and nourishment to the poor, the weak, the disenfranchised; the return of the grail to American Capital.

The Flamingo, on the other hand, was entirely Ben Siegel's idea. In his desert rapture he dreamed up everything we mean when we say Las Vegas, and though he never saw it realized, he came closer to getting what he wanted than Roosevelt did. In spite of a disastrous opening on the night after Christmas, 1946, when practically no one from L.A. showed up (George Raft was one of the few exceptions, driving the three hundred miles through freak storms that had closed the L.A. airports, and against the orders of the studio bosses, who in turn were responding to pressure from William Randolph Hearst to boycott the Flamingo); in spite of heavy losses for the house during the first six months, nothing could reduce his faith in the hotel. He believed in it against common sense, against counsel from his stockholders and increasingly unambiguous warnings, until the warnings stopped, and he, of all people, could see what was coming. He just believed in it even more then, faithful right up to the minute that they came down from headquarters and shot him, making sure to put a couple into those blue eyes, so that everyone who saw the papers next day would understand that this one was personal. Twenty minutes later, the stockholders walked in and took over the Flamingo.

◆

Ninety-nine men lost their lives in the construction of Boulder Dam, and for years there was the strange but popular belief, that the bodies of those men were buried inside the dam, as though the United States Government would have stood still for such a thing. There's no way of knowing how many lives were lost during the building of the Flamingo and its aftermath, or where those bodies might be buried, since all of those costs were well under the table and occurred, like Siegel's death in Beverly Hills, out of town and across state lines, and were strictly intramural. ("We only kill each other," Siegel used to say.) Whether considered as works of art or as generators of the new life, Boulder and Flamingo were very expensive projects. All these years later, there's hardly anyone around who would suggest that they were too expensive.

It's appropriate, even romantic, that the two men should have passed each other here in the corridors outside the big room, where F.D.R.'s search for less and less class intersected Ben Siegel's search for more and more. Except in historical hallucination, of course, there's no possibility that the two men ever actually met, or even appeared for a moment together in the same place. But it's certain that on several occasions, F.D.R. shook a hand that shook the hand of Bugsy Siegel. A dubious relationship, but, skin being skin and non-retractable, a definite connection.

JIMMY DURANTE

Did you ever have the feeling
that you wanted to go,
And still you have the feeling
that you wanted to stay . . .

Plenty of stars have opened in Las Vegas, but only one opened Las Vegas itself, on that dismal first night of the Flamingo, when show business crossed the desert and Jimmy Durante played to probably the smallest audience of his career.

Most likely he agreed to make the benediction as a favor to Ben Siegel. In the days when they were both coming up, fewer distinctions got made about the various sides of the law and who stood where, or with whom. When the lower east side fell on Broadway, when Broadway was Broadway and Jimmy Durante was its best-loved star, the acts and the mugs ran around together all the time. When he was fronting and performing at the Club Durant, the biggest names in town came every night to sit in the field of his benevolent rage, proud to have him pull their tables away from them to throw across the stage at the bandleader. They'd reach out and try to touch that magic schnozz for luck, for the autograph, while the club's real owners sat upstairs counting the money, and downstairs, in the garage, Arnold

Rothstein ran the wildest poker game in New York. "I'm surrounded by assassins!" was the gag, arms akimbo in indignation then dropped to the sides in resignation. But Jimmy Durante was living proof that not everyone who lies down with the dogs gets up with the fleas.

◆

Jimmy the Well Dressed Man, destroyer of pianos and syntaxes, pure performing essence of the immigrant will at its most fierce and bewildered. With a little bit of this-a and a little bit of that-a, a little Papageno in his youth, a little Malvolio through the middle, not a little Prospero in old age, Umbriago all the way. Old people and little children loved him. That release of maximum aggression with none of the damage, over and over, made everyone feel happy, and no one was ever unmoved by the ritual finish of his act, stepping away through diminishing receding spotlights like a man with enormous visible dignity (and great reserves of dignity besides), practicing for his own death and signing off, "Goodnight Mrs. Calabash, wherever you are ..."

◆

They loved him from coast to coast, but on the coasts they loved him most of all.

These were the conditions that prevailed: Whenever he was in New York where most of the

Goodnight, Mrs. Calabash. *1978*

work and much of his heart lay, his family in L.A. wanted him home. So he would go back to L.A., and his agent would pressure him to return to New York. Pulled this way and that way then vice-versa, he was on the horns of a dilemma. But on the Super Chief and the Twentieth Century he could have what he wanted, a little peace and quiet, and nobody but the porter got into the act.

So let's celebrate,
Gee I'm feeling great,
I'm the guy who found the lost chord.

HOOT GIBSON

A strange thing happened to this old cowpoke, he rode straight into a warp. A real, working cowboy, he went into the movies and played cowboys, and after a few years of that he was believable as a cowboy only on the screen.

But he didn't like Hollywood, and he couldn't really go back to the bunkhouse and the prairie. It seemed like he didn't belong anywhere, so he moved here, bought a little spread outside of town, and lived into old age like a grounded Ghost Rider In The Sky.

The Last Outlaw. 1978

BETTY HUTTON

Even a child could see that something was wrong, Betty Hutton folded tight in the arms of her leading man, her eyes as soft and clouded with passion as Bergman's, or Dietrich's. It was easy to believe that she was in love with him, but not that he was in love with her.

◆

If you're taking the bombshell route, you're only supposed to go off

A Quiet Afternoon. *1978*

once, on impact, but she sustained explosion for ten or twelve years. She was like the blond you saw or read about in Winchell, who made a spectacle of herself in a night-club and, animated by the sensation she caused, did it every night until people stopped looking, and the clubs stopped letting her in. The national frenzy she embodied and acted out so relentlessly changed its character as soon as those damned guitars started up, and became other frenzies that she couldn't jitter jump and jive to. They say she found a measure of peace after career-death, working as a servant to a servant of the Lord.

◆

In one of her films she played twins. One was brunette, demure and reserved, and the other was a blond, extremely manic. The blond we already knew, but the dark sister was a surprise, more attractive, much more restful. It was almost like watching two actresses working. In the most complimentary sense, a little of her went a long way. She really found her range in that one. It makes you wonder, maybe she was too subtle for us after all.

CONRAD HILTON

A latter day tycoon, a manufacturing genius almost on a par with Ford, but whose product was a nice place to lay down your tired head, no matter where you were. His name stood for standardized accommodation, once so berated by classical-humanist hotel lovers, now so familiar, reassuring, desirable. A room at the Hilton bore the same relation to heart's ease that the white paper band around the toilet bears to hygiene.

Hilton liked to stay at the Hilton himself, in the Emperor Suite, and to dance the Versoviana in the "Grand" ballroom until the early hours. The Versoviana was a dance he made up himself, since no dance existed that completely satisfied his requirements for old-world grace, romance and elegance.

Air Conditioning. 1979

NICK THE GREEK

"There was a kind of faded elegance about Nicholos Dandolos in the final years of his life. He was like a once-rich European aristocrat, living in an empty mansion. The servants were gone. Drop cloths covered what was left of the furniture. The electricity had been turned off. But he still dressed for dinner every night."

— Jimmy the Greek

"The greatest experience in life is winning a bet, and the second greatest is losing one."

— Nick the Greek

The Gambler. 1977

NOËL COWARD

In the afternoons, he said, he liked to stare out of the windows of his room at the Sands and dream about the redskins and covered wagons which the view suggested to him. Nights, he went downstairs and knocked the people dead.

Just a song at twilight. You don't get much further from Mayfair than this, but not even Mayfair ever gave Noël Coward more adoration. They were mad about him, so insouciant and soigné, and such a good sport.

His success opened the doors of the big room to so many class and even European acts, that the punters hardly knew the old place. Ben Siegel would have been wild with pride: It was the Augustan Age of Las Vegas.

A Song at Twilight. *1977*

TALLULAH BANKHEAD

Speaking of the class acts, Tallulah Bankhead and Marlene Dietrich once played Las Vegas in the same week.

"I hear that Marlene paid $7,000 for her gown," Tallulah said. "Personally, I believe that anybody who pays more than $5,000 for a gown is out of their head."

Giants Drop Six Straight Ball Games. *1978*

WALTER WINCHELL

Hemingway called him "a terrible little pro", his victims and enemies, of whom there were so many, called him a vicious two-faced coward, and he called himself "the man who invented the low blow." In the first stage of the ongoing war against what used to be called "private life", WW was Julius Caesar, devising and perfecting through daily repetition over thirty years, the basic techniques still used today. Although his Commentaries are no longer read or even much remembered, he established levels of intrusive outrage that were monumental for their time, and that those of us living now in The Age Of Candor have found hard to maintain.

As a vaudevillian he was strictly a deuce act, never rising above the second spot on the bill in the second circuit. His dancing was aggressive but without grace or timing, his singing was nasal and piercing, and as a comic, although he would show the world that he had no equal in snappy patter, good humor wasn't in him. The only good thing about his career as an entertainer was that it got him backstage, and since his eyes weren't blinded by the bright lights or his ears deafened by applause, he kept them open, taut. Rejected so thoroughly by vaudeville, he left and took vaudeville with him into journalism, where he became a headliner. He was as famous as any star, rich as a tycoon, more powerful than almost any politician, and when he had achieved all of that he reached his hand down to his brothers and sisters in show business, and made them eat out of it.

◆

He could walk in and see F.D.R. almost any time he felt like it, which is more than Eleanor could do, and the publicity he lavished on J. Edgar Hoover and his obscure, starving little agency put the FBI on the map, on top of the map, and all over the map. Some of the orchids he sent had a longer life than any orchids we could send, and he made a lot of careers by sending them, broke careers by withholding them. His rare retractions were invariably more damaging than the original item, as the actress found out when she complained to him about being reported dead in his column. He was quick to apologize. "Josephine Sexton is alive, she says."

Everybody read him, listened to him on the radio, tried to keep on the right side of him. With so many sources, he was inevitably mistaken for the Source. By a coalition of luck and instinct and a lack of shame, he was perfectly placed in the information flow of his day, the human wire stretched across the country and the age that

he did as much as anybody to define. The terminal was table 50 at The Stork Club, where the supplicants came nervously sweating, chafing against the velvet rope, straining for eye-contact, praying for the sign to step forward, bend the knee, and spill. And the next morning we all had the item, Mr. and Mrs. America and all the ships at sea. The items were our common denominator, the columns came to be lifelines, as interest turned to fascination, and fascination turned to obsession. In the annals of addiction, nobody ever turned more people on than Walter Winchell.

◆

"I want to get back at a lot of people. If I drop dead before I get to the Z's in the alphabet, you'll know how I hated to go." He lived too long into the time when nobody needed him anymore. The demand that he created was so extreme that new outlets and methods were developed, and he was completely lost in them. All that the people who watched him on television could see was an angry old guy with his hat on, yelling at the camera. The Stork Club was gone, Roosevelt was long gone, most of the once-powerful papers that he wrote for were gone (including his flagship, The New York Daily Mirror), and nearly all of the great contributions that Mencken and the Algonquin crowd always said he had made to the American language had gone phffft and dropped back out of use again, but he couldn't leave the stage. He'd never lost the itch, the old Lion of Broadway; all his life he could always be seen front-row center, ringside, or standing in the wings looking wistfully at the talent.

Broadway Booth. 1984

Poolside with Charo. *1977*

XAVIER CUGAT

It's only the tango you love …

We dance to the music of love, your heart beats with mine as we sway, from the Roof of the Waldorf to Culver City, dancing the tango, the conga, the pericon; the beguine, the samba, the mamba, the rumbas (son and danson), the bolero and the maxixe. Musically and visually, Cugie's act was one of a kind, pure glamour.

And always the latest Mrs. Cugat, *mucha mujera*, up there singing with the orchestra. Always a Latin (if only from Manhattan), he always married them, they always left him, and he always found another one, younger and wilder, to shake the maracas and chalakas and drive all the old men crazy.

JOE DIMAGGIO

No heroes without adversity.

"Old injuries have caught up with me, and I've had new ones ..." he said, announcing his retirement from baseball in December, 1951. Not the least of these injuries was a depression, aggravated by his unhappy marriage to a starlet named Dorothy Arnold.

He had hit the long ball clean and truly, but it took a bad hop. In his room at the Hotel Edison, he packed his bags, stopped to adjust his suspenders so that his cuffs hung evenly, and left for California to translate and extend his heroism into other fields.

End of the Season. 1979 43

MILTON BERLE

"Whoever said that nothing is impossible never tried to get between Milton Berle and a television camera."

Somebody had to go first. Nobody knew in those days what the tolerances were, or what the effects of concentrated, repeated exposure might be on the body, the central nervous system, the mind. A man had to be found who combined the resourcefulness of a frontier scout with the stamina of an astronaut, to run himself through the system once and perform the still incredibly dangerous ceremony known as Topping The Ratings. He got the job by virtue of his energy, appetite, nerve and sheer availability. And knowledge.

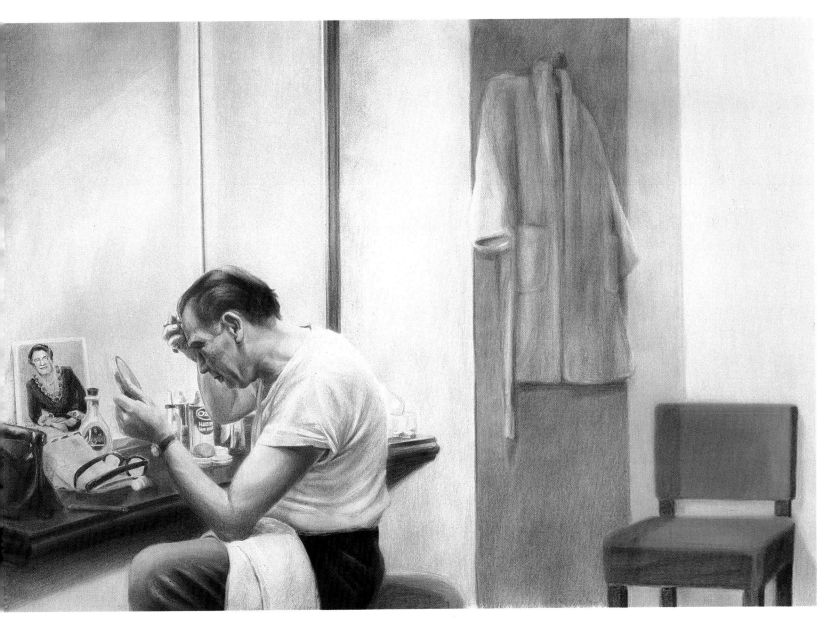

The Comedian. *1977*

By the time the call came in 1947, he'd been learning ten jokes a day for nearly thirty years, and over the next five seasons, he did them all.

The Thief of Bad Gags (he laughed so hard at Jack Benny he almost dropped his pencil, etc.), he was plainly no mere thief. He was more of an archivist, the processor and transmitter of every low gag, cheap laugh, cockamamie bit, juvenile stunt, triple take, borschtbelt vulgarity and slapstick indignity that had ever dared show itself on any stage: Tent show, medicine show, minstrel/carnival/burlesque/vaudeville/nightclub show, all the American shows that had ever gone on before this moment, when they were all brought in together under one ceiling over the biggest room that anyone had ever played, and to an audience never imagined before, not only in its numbers, but in its nature.

◆

This was the last possible moment of hesitation. With Milton Berle came the great leap forward in television sales. ("I know I sold mine," Joe E. Lewis said, "and my brother sold his.") The coaxial cable was still moving west, a more fateful line than the railroad a hundred years before, but in the irradiant east on Tuesday nights between eight and nine, you knew what almost everybody was doing. The movie theatres, restaurants and clubs were empty, Broadway curtains were held, and the taverns were packed, everyone leaning on the bar the same way, looking at the same thing. Families asked the neighbors in, we sat together in the gravid shadows with our backs to the radio, and we couldn't believe what we were seeing. Already amazed to be living in the Atomic Age, we let our poor imaginations lead us into thinking that this was just another wrinkle, an evolution, that we were watching shrunken movies, or some kind of radio-with-pictures. And we felt that it was a full life in the greatest country on earth that offered the rich and poor alike something as wonderful as this, the proposition we'd waited centuries for, new lamps for old.

"Oh Jesus," my father groaned. "That's an old one."
"I never heard it before," I answered.

Every time we saw him we couldn't wait to see him again, and in the new way, forming himself out of that flat depthless darkness; "a man with no shame", in a gorilla suit, a Santa suit, a zoot suit, dressed up like the Easter Bunny or in drag, teeth blacked out, with rubber ears and feet; coming God knows how out of the strangely-charged dot of green light, (David Sarnoff's *ignis fatuus*, a green with no name, that had never been seen before), performing a volume of his epic encyclopedia of American show business, and disappearing back into the dot again. It was always true of the greatest performers that they took a piece of us with them when they finished. Why was this any different?

Times change, but this wasn't quite the same thing. From the minute you had a set in your house, the hours, days and weeks fastened themselves around the screen. Tuesday night received the husk of the old week and teleported the full body of the new. Wednesdays were for replay. In the schoolyard, at the bus stop, over the lunch counter and down at the shop, all the gags that were old or dead were young again, not only living but back in circulation, and in this way it was absolutely true that Milton Berle was on all the time.

MARILYN MONROE

Flesh Impact

LAS VEGAS, NEV.
MAY 25th, 1946

… I'm having lots of rest and I'm getting a tan. It's very warm and honestly the sun shines all the time.
Roy Rogers was in town making a picture. I met him and rode his horse Trigger (cross my heart I did!). What a horse! … Ever since, I've been signing autograph books and cowboy hats. When I try and tell these kids I'm not in pictures they think I'm trying to avoid signing their books, so I sign them.
They've gone now. It's quite lonely here in Las Vegas. This is certainly a wild town …

Her lines formed the Receptive, which many took to mean the Receptacle. They say that in her starlet years the powerful and pretend powerful of Hollywood used her as often and carefully as a piece of Kleenex. But they also say that it didn't embitter her, or, (obviously), cheapen her. She stood for us above the usual and vulgar implications of the act like a child, inviolate and inadequate, and kept to herself the opening they never penetrated, or even found.

She made it up into the godworld, and the place was impossible. Raised so high with no self to sustain her, she shook and leaned and grasped for support, and there was never enough. Lots of

Certainly a Wild Town. 1986

times she pulled herself into some kind of shape to function, but she couldn't hold it for long, she couldn't get any rest from her sleep, and so she went out, into her fabulous afterlife.

You hear about someone carrying a torch for years, but this is the first time the torch ever got handed on to the next generation. It leaves you feeling that whatever or whoever killed Marilyn Monroe didn't do a very thorough job of it. She still just has to walk into the room and you're down on your knees again.

JIMMY HOFFA

Nobody is really larger than life. Only people who think their own lives are small could ever believe that.

He was, to be ambivalent if not charitable, like his union, "A Part of the American Life." He stood for a better standard of living for the working man and his family, was a great family man himself; and a boss, a matchmaker, a banker and town-planner, the visible part of an invisible government run "on the cantilever principal," as Dos Passos put it, "through interlocking directorates"; a hard man, a man with many admirers and enemies (often the same people), and a man

The President. *1978*

with his own private code, which he drew on to keep order below while he worked endlessly on his brutal, awesome tapestry, woven out of all the strands of Ends and Means that he could grab, and hold. And while some of the boys thought he was getting "too flaky to run things anymore", he did a hundred pushups a day to keep his arms strong, and went on – his greatness as a conspirator can't be appreciated enough – conspiring with his own people to uplift them and degrade them. Mainly a dealer in services, he was no stranger to supply-side.

He paid his debt to society two years short of the five year sentence, coming out into the not very open air in a "welter" of rumors, gossip, plots and shaky cover stories. He moved quickly to put things back the way they'd been, but he didn't have it anymore. Once, if he couldn't take a thing with his fists, his incredibly subtle wrist would get it. For a smart guy, he forgot an awful lot; precepts, procedures, good advice and stronger: such as the words that Anthony "Tony Pro" Provenzano said to him in the Lewisburg Prison yard as they were being pulled off of each other, "Old man! Yours is coming! You know it's coming one of these days."

SUGAR RAY ROBINSON

A piece of spontaneous oral Hemingway occurred at a training camp in Watertown, New York in 1940 between a local sportswriter and a fight manager.

"That's a sweet boy you have there," the sportswriter said.

"Sweet as sugar," the manager replied.

◆

Sweet in name, sweet in deed, sweet in memory, which in this case doesn't lie. Archive footage will support the wildest nostalgias about him; the most adroit, most adept, most stylish; the greatest boxer who ever lived. Pound for pound, of course. There was never anybody the hipsters loved to watch fight more than Gentleman Sugar Ray.

When he was ten years old in Detroit, he used to go to the Brewster Center Gym to watch an amateur boxer named Joe Louis work out. In 1951, when Ray was negotiating for what he believed he was worth, and refusing to box unless he got it, the International Boxing Commission sent Louis around to appeal to him to back down. Ray shook his head in disbelief. "How can *you* ask me to do that," he said, "after what they did to you?" Louis had been a popular champion, for a black man. After Sugar Ray, there would be different kinds of popular champions.

◆

Unfortunately his other reputation, as a shrewd businessman, was inflated. He lost two fortunes, including four million in purses, a block in Harlem, and a number of other interests, through bad judgement, through treachery, through his generosity and the common drainage that goes with entourage maintenance, although he himself lived quite simply, fuchsia Cadillac and the wardrobe notwithstanding.

◆

"Put that in," a promoter said (a man who probably lost a bundle on Ray). "No matter what they say about the guy, he never put on a bad show anyplace in the world."

After his first retirement, he tried show business. In 1952 he was getting $ 15,000 a week in Vegas. But he had a strange and uncomfortable reverence for showbiz, and no opponent between himself and the audience through which to ex-

Harlem Nocturne. *1978*

press his irreproachable form. His act was a stage adaptation of the visible part of his training, not the most interesting part. Finally it was only very sharp training and didn't lead to anything. His fees dropped to $ 5,000 a week, and he went back into the ring after two years to become a great champion again.

◆

Years after it was all over, he was honored with an evening in Madison Square Garden. He stood in the center of the ring, while four of the men he'd beaten stood in the corners: Gene Fullmer, Bobo Olson, Randy Turpin and Carmine Basilio. It's probably silly to say that they ever felt it had been a privilege to have been messed up so politely by him, although they must have appreciated the style with which he'd done it to them. It's a sure thing though that once a man had been in the ring with Sugar Ray, he was spoiled for any other fighter. In this, they had something in common with the women who had been at various times partners with Fred Astaire, pound for pound the greatest dancer of them all.

LIBERACE

Have a thought for the apparently large portion of the audience who might never have found their entertainment if it hadn't have been for him. Their devotion to him, and to his regalia, is reflected by the yearly gate at the Liberace Museum in Las Vegas, which he impishly refers to as an "expensive joke", something like his career, as he might be the first to concede. Of course there's more to it than mere tack, but (even though he is not normally associated with modesty), he never talks about it.

Once, when he was a young pianist starting out in the lounges, some hood insulted his playing, and he burst into tears. He never let anything like that happen again. Later, he turned a few people's heads around, and drew strong public attention to options of behavior that were, believe it or not, unspoken of and almost unheard of in most parts of the country. Never before, at least knowingly, had a man ever had the big steel balls to show himself like that, and on television. We know how much the jokes hurt him at first, and how he dealt with it. Besides, just because a man acts like a pansy doesn't make him a sissy. For all of that cruelty, he's had remuneration and restitution, laughing all the way to the bank, and more last laughs than a piano has keys.

The Loved One. 1978

JAYNE MANSFIELD

"I'm a big girl and I have to have a big guy," the Whore of Babylon said. "I love to be loved back, real strong."

She was inches ahead of the competition, the hood ornament on the unstoppable forward-rolling vehicle of the "new permission", flashing that little-girl smile, and that crazy body. "She's got a lot of what they call the Most," as the song about her said.

Too vulgar, too much, publicity-mad both ways: mad for publicity and driven mad by her publicity. She never knew when to stop, how to stop, or even that stopping was something you had to do when fame was all you ever wanted, or all you'd ever get. ("The girl can't help it," the song went on, "The girl can't help it.")

It wasn't going too well. Second Marilyn Monroes were a dime a gross, only the original was rare, and Jayne just went on leading with the tits, clammy and ubiquitous as a fog over America, and the smile looked a bit deranged, even terrified. She never thought we'd get this bored, or turn so cold, once we had what we wanted from her. She was treated like a freak, even death treated her that way. Then there was only her husband, Mickey Hargitay, Mr. Universe of 1955, to stand by her memory, making like Joe Dimaggio with the grief and the flowers and the never-ending love.

Trying On. 1986

JUDY GARLAND

"Not every end is a goal.

The end of a melody is not its goal; however, if the melody has not reached its end, it
would also not have reached its goal. A parable."

— Nietzsche

The Palladium. 1985

JOE E. LEWIS

"My friends all tell me, 'Joe,
You drink too much, your life you're losing'.
But they're all dead, and I'm still here,
Alive and boozing.
I know I drank a lot,
Threw up on every highway,
I was a souse,
But not a louse,
I did it my way."

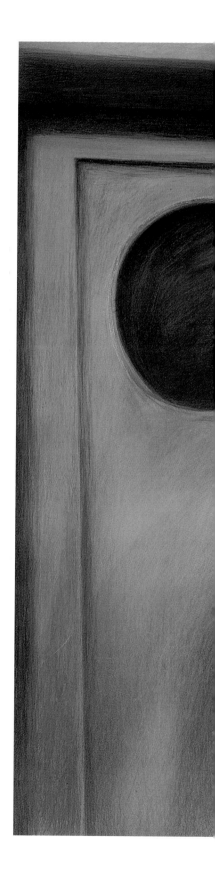

Lord, You Made the Night Too Long. *1978*

MARIO LANZA

The Mario Lanza Story comes to us with all the unerring perfection-seeking stranger than fiction cosmetic action of a studio publicity handout. It's true enough that all biography is to some extent a fiction, but in this case it's hard to see through the technicolor distortion, and decide which night was the loveliest night of the year, or even which year it might have occurred in.

Picture a scene, Alfred Arnold Cocozza, a little boy singing along with his father's Caruso records in the poor part of town, born the same year that Caruso died, coming to adolescence believing that there hadn't been room on the planet for both of them, and even that he was Caruso reincarnate, until the fade out / fade in to a grown, robust man singing the role he knew he was born to sing, and making millions think so too. (Although others said he was a rank impersonator, Placido Domingo has said of Lanza that the voice was there; comparisons of the voices alone were not as ludicrous as many people said. But, he added, a great voice alone is only a voice. Like a great pitching arm without the eye and the timing, or an angel-face concealing demons.)

Imagine next the singing truck driver, but do it quickly, because he only worked on the trucks for ten days. Referring to the handout, we see that on that tenth day he was delivering a piano to the Philadelphia Academy of Music when he burst into song, and the great Koussevitsky ran shirtless and shoeless from his dressing room, maybe, to see where that glorious voice was coming from.

Or hear him on that magical night when he sang an aria from *Andrea Chenier* in the Hollywood Bowl, and in the audience, possibly, was Louis B. Mayer, who leapt to his feet with everyone else and joined in the twelve (ten, two) minute ovation, signing him the next morning to an MGM contract. After that, it took them two years to find a property suited to his peculiar talents, and looks. Then, at the moment of his fullest success, his devils came in from the wings, and he sang only with them afterwards. Within five years of his first fame he was left singing alone behind a screen while a handsome juvenile mouthed the words to the camera, because nobody needed or wanted a 300 pound Student Prince.

By the time of his big comeback attempt, in Las Vegas, he had gained and lost and regained more weight than is good for anybody, least of all tenors, whose hearts are routinely subjected to such strain that it was said of one tenor who died

My Name is Cocozza. 1977

on stage that Verdi had killed him. Lanza's records still sold in the millions, his fans remembered and loved him. His salary was the highest ever offered to any star in Vegas, the house was packed, but he never made it to the stage. "Due to illness," the release read, and it was perfectly true. Pills and alcohol, usual enough in jazz and rock and roll but rare in opera circles, had left him frozen in the doorway of his dressing room. A few months later, he was dead.

RED SKELTON

In the early 1800s, the story goes, a man arrived at the London surgery of a famous specialist in nervous disorders. He complained to the doctor of listlessness, exhaustion, nightmares and a chronic, deepening melancholia.

"This is really quite simple," the doctor told him. "You must seek out laughter and diversion. For example, why don't you go to the theatre tonight and see the clown Grimaldi perform? I'm told that he is extremely amusing."

"Yes," the man said, "but I *am* Grimaldi."

Venice. 1986

HOWARD HUGHES

No, you're right, that's him. Look fast, don't even blink, and look hard, since you won't be getting another chance. It may not be an honor or a pleasure, but it's certainly a distinction. "Those who say they see him don't, and those who see him don't say," so mum's the word. And don't for Christ sake wait around for him to say hello. Look and go.

◆

He used to get around a lot, but that was before. Before exactly *what* is the real mystery that all the other mysteries come out of, but something must have happened to age him thirty years between the time he was thirty-five and forty-five, to make him want to turn himself into a ghost, The Phantom of the Opera of American Power. A fabled lover of either sex, he grew not just tired of but phobic about other people's skin, and morbid with his own. The players' player, he's up there now in the Desert Inn penthouse getting weirder and weirder: not a thousand feet from the center of the action, he never goes down to see it. It's forbidden to touch him.

Maybe there are no second acts in most American lives, but this one had the hat-size to run out to the full five, like Lear: full of dukes turned (or re-turned) to treachery, the kingdom divided and the king a prisoner or completely gaa or both, and no one close enough to be Fool, and no one good enough to play Cordelia, to soften or crack the great heart; not even one among the hundreds who'd been under his personal contract. (And then not just the starlets, but the escorts, and the private eyes to make sure that the escorts didn't lay a finger on the starlets, with a second private eye out in the parking lot to watch the first, and sometimes a third private eye to watch the others. You can't say that Howard Hughes didn't have a world view.)

Sure, you hear stories, about how he sits up there all the time watching old movies over and over, how he's a hemoglobin vampire, even how he slips out alone late at night and walks in the desert wearing empty Kleenex boxes on his feet. Maybe they're better than shoes for walking on sand, and anyway, that's his business. It's his life, and if he can't live it the way he wants, who can?

◆

"Everyone says that Hughes is in excellent health," said Nevada Governor O'Callaghan. "But they always add that if he saw any of our people it would be traumatic. The two statements don't jibe. What's so traumatic about seeing someone?"

Vision. 1976

Bus Station. *1976*

LENNY BRUCE

He's crazy

> *Zug nicht … tsi gurnischt … patamunzo …*
> *verbisener … bubeh misah …*

He's a wierdo

> *"What is he? What's 'schmuck'? He keeps*
> *saying 'schmuck', and 'pootz', 'pout',*
> *'poots', 'parts' … and, and 'bread', 'cool',*
> *'dig', 'schmooz', 'grap', 'pup', 'schlluup',*
> *'mugh' …"*

He's on the dope

> *"I dunno what the hell he's talking about."*
> *"You like him?"*
> *"I wanna go to the toilet."*
> *"Awright … I'll go with you."*
> *"I don't wanna walk in front of him."*
> *"Pootz, brootz, mugrup, blog …"*

If you bombed in Las Vegas, at the tables or in your act (if, for example, you talked filth, or were one of those comics who made the band laugh but never the audience), the house would give you a bus ticket for the other side of the nearest state line, a loser being a worse liability than broken tubing in a neon display; if you wanted to kill yourself, better you did it in California. You were compensated anyway, because when you boarded the bus you were a pariah, but when you got off the bus at the other end you were not.

> *… tumler … schtuck-schtick … schpritz …*
> *kugel … emmis … schmecker … schtup …*
> *emmis … verfallen, emmis …*

> *"Yeah, I guess I'm really getting to be a bring-*
> *down. But it's this* town *that does it.*

NAT KING COLE

There's a sentimental belief that in the big room there are many rooms, but this has never been proven and is unlikely, if not frankly impossible.

◆

Nat King Cole entered the mainstream like quicksilver from a faraway place to become a major crossover act. Before Elvis Presley, who was half crossed-over to begin with, Cole was the most successful example of the phenomenon. In fact, his career probably established Crossover as a real, enduring show business principle, by introducing not only a black performer of unyielding reserve to white mass culture, but by introducing a most understated jazz intention to material that seemed absolutely jazzproof, so that a vast adoring audience never *had* to know that they had been listening to jazz at all.

A lot of inadequate language has been spent by people attempting to describe his voice. It was called sultry and crisp, it was compared to smoke, honey, velvet and silk; it glistened like his eyes when he sang, a love-whisper perfectly enunciated, burnished, making sounds like rain on your window when you're glad and rain on your window when you're sad. Yet when you hear his records, he really doesn't sound like any of these things. Billy Eckstine cut through this by observing that Nat King Cole "took a style, and made a voice of it." The style, at least, is describable.

He found it on the piano first, and it was fully formed before he ever sang. It was a club

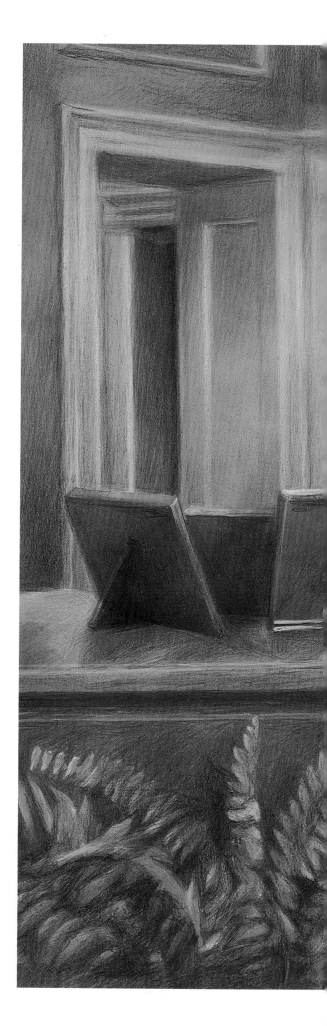

Melancholy Monarch. 1984

style, West Coast jazz club and bandbox. (The story goes that it was a persistent drunk in a night-club, a big (three-dollar) tipper demanding "Sweet Lorraine", that made him first sing in pub-lic, rhyming "baby boy" with "choo-choo choy", satisfying the drunk's requirements and his own.) It's a subtle and difficult style to master, and, since its most precious quality is intimacy, an al-most impossible style to bring into the big room. In a big room situation, you would find out very quickly who was impeccable, and who was not. Because of him, songs that had practically no right to live became ineradicable. Sung within the protection of that style they were transformed, like subverted rubbish, falling on white ears like delicate blossoms, with shi-fa fa on the side, tacit and delicious.

◆

Over the years, hundreds of jazz and R & B acts have played Las Vegas: Louis Arm-strong, Benny Goodman, Duke Ellington, Louis Jordan, Count Basie and Nat King Cole among them. They played their sets and made the people happy. Most of them took as much from the place as they brought to it. Still, it might be nice to imagine that after the show they met together someplace less public, in some fabulous desert dream of Smokey Joe's, where they played for each other, and played only what they felt like playing.

MARLENE DIETRICH

In "Morocco"

"I felt it might be interesting to have Amy Jolly, during a singing routine, kiss a female member of the audience on the lips. Von Stern-berg said, 'The studio might censor it.' 'Okay,' I replied, 'then we'll have Amy take a rose from the woman, carry it across the room, and give it to the legionnaire. That way, they'll have to let the kiss stay in. Otherwise, people will say, 'Where did the rose come from?'"

Ich hab' noch einen Koffer in Berlin. *1977*

GEORGE RAFT

"If dames are a crime,
then I'm guilty as hell."

Whenever the Hollywood blue-noses criticized him for some of the company he kept, he'd say, "What am I supposed to do, not shake hands with a guy?" or, "I say hello to everyone who says hello to me." He didn't expect anyone to buy it, but then, he didn't really care.

The fact is, they all went back a long way together, even before he first came out of Hell's Kitchen to star in the top clubs, dancing the bolero, the tango, and the Charleston, when Broadway was the center of the world, so long ago that Al Capone was still calling himself Brown. Arnold Rothstein, Legs Diamond, Owney Madden

Night After Night. 1981

(Raft once drove a beer truck for Madden), Charley Lucky, Dutch Schultz; he knew them all, and he didn't high-hat them later, when he made it big in pictures. But that's the kind of guy he was. George Raft didn't take shit from anybody, never asked a favor for himself, and never turned his back on a friend. Not like the rest of that bunch out there.

"They all had Dusenbergs and 16-cylinder Cadillacs, and, like somebody said, when there was money around you might step on some of it."

One of his best friends was Ben Siegel. They'd known each other at least since the early days of the Bug and Meyer Mob, possibly since they were boys. Siegel took a great many things from his friend; some said his whole Hollywood style: the wardrobe, the patter, the moves, the way he looked at men, the way he looked at women, and at least a hundred thousand dollars, which he threw desperately, madly, into the sinking Flamingo Hotel. Raft could say and do things to Siegel that nobody else would have gotten away with. One Christmas he sent him a toupee, knowing how touchy Bugsy was about his thinning hair. Siegel sped across Beverly Hills and threw it in Raft's face.

"I oughtta kill you for that," he screamed.

"Take it easy, Baby Blue Eyes," George Raft said.

♦

"Hoover! I knew the guy! I introduced him to the Aly Khan at DelMar Racetrack."

When Siegel went down still owing him a fortune, or when the IRS climbed all over him, or J. Edgar Hoover conspired with the British Home Office to keep Raft from ever returning to his London casino on the grounds that he was an undesirable alien, he took it standing up. Even when old age came and his box-office slipped, sending him through what for any other leading man would have been the movie-star hells of self-parody and character parts, he didn't bend.

♦

In *I'll Get You For This*, a very late film, he and his leading lady are caught out on the dancefloor just as the foxtrot ends and a tango begins. She laughs nervously.

"Do you tango?" she asks him.

"I used to," George Raft says, and right there on the night-club floor he takes her in an adagio so strong, fluent and steady that for a moment you're not sure whether what you're seeing is the tango itself or the action that the tango was always meant to remind you of.

JOE LOUIS

Just Another Lucky Night

In 1970, Joe Louis went to work for Caesar's Palace as the hotel's Official Greeter. It was a logical move. He was a born dignitary, and he'd been an employee of sorts all his life. Even at its height, his glory had an aspect that was ceremonial, on behalf of syndicated interests; white cash and black hope, both repaid with dividends. So many backers, so many friends (so many in need), but he was the one who had to move alone across the surface of his own time, and cause the changes. The center of the action was his center too, and it was filled with his great qualities. The main one was a sense of purpose that cut through greed and hatred, so that even the people who came to root for Max Schmeling were inspired when Louis beat him in less than one round. There had never been an All-American Negro before Joe Louis. There hadn't even been that concept.

For a few years, it was the fashion among both races to say that he'd been a fool. Sportswriters, with the sentimental grandiloquence that cheapened every thrill, had written about his Samson-in-the-Temple routine for fifteen years. Broke, and caught in overlapping tax nightmares, he was ostensibly "reduced" to performing as a professional wrestler. There had been disgrace, mental illness and addiction, but if he was in chains, they were invisible, even to the press. He was much too substantial to be the shadow of his former self that everyone expected to see. They never dreamed that they'd actually stand so close to the real Joe Louis, absorbing his fabulous left-right combinations in every handshake and pat on the back. Feeling unusually brave, they took the fresh taste of that risk to the tables with them and left him there on the hotel steps, a classic grounded in his old strengths, the gravity that money couldn't buy and the knowledge that money couldn't erase.

Daylight. *1977*

MARTIN AND LEWIS

If we're just talking story here, this one plays like a dream. It's got period, it's got show-biz, it's got rivalry and buddylove, music, laughter, big success and a beautiful shape. It's all there. Up to a point.

◆

Pals, partners, soulmates, they were the biggest Double in history.

The singer had been getting by okay on his own, and once the wiseguys fronted him the dough to get his nose bobbed he really started taking off, a big hit in the small rooms, but with a following. Five or six more years of it and he might have become big. The comic, however, was perpetrating a "record act" – a phonograph record played behind the curtain, while he spazzed and mugged around – the lowest act in show business. But from time to time their paths would cross in the clubs, and something happened between them; the smoothie and the shmeggegie, the crooner and the kid and, for spice, the Italo-Judeo kicker. Together they were hilarious, but there was tenderness between them too, and they took it to the top. So far so good.

Their phenomenal success only seemed to strengthen the bond. But then the planet that governs friendship, or ego, or money and power, went into a bad position, and what had always been so much fun turned into hard work. Maybe one of them secretly thought that he was carrying the other, or one of them feared that he was being carried by the other. Then, at the turn, the suspicions and resentments were reversed, and there are some reversals that not even the closest partnership can stand. Rumors of a split started leaking out, more titillating than if it had been an old Hollywood marriage. Then the breakup, and

Pardners. 1985

people taking sides. Most of them backed the comic – the antic, to be more accurate – against the crooner-straightman, and a lot of bones got chipped when they saw how wrong they'd been and stampeded to change back again.

So for many years, they don't speak. They hate to be reminded of the team they used to be, yet any time one of them does a guest shot, the host brings it up. They avoid gatherings where they might run into each other. But everybody thinks that inside, they're still crazy about each other. It's been eating both of them, but they're too proud to make a move.

Then someone, the biggest star of all, who's pals with both of them, and powerful enough to get away with it, gets an idea. He sets it up so that one night, after all those years, they're surprised together on a stage, reunion by ambush. The cheers and tears are too much for them. Shocked into reconciliation, they stand apart, look, remember who and where they are, get that old feeling, and fall into each other's arms.

There's your ending, pull way back and fade on that. Never mind that when it was over they both went home alone, or that what really went on inside the circle of the spotlight was as complicated, emotional, layered and long as War and Peace, put together.

BOB HOPE

December, 1967. A reporter remembers:

They'd fixed up a corner of the Command helicopter with pillows to make the short ride more comfortable for him. He strapped in, had a word with his producer, and then, as the rotors started, he stuffed cotton into his ears and leaned back. Before the ship had reached a thousand feet he was out. He wasn't sleeping deeply. He was resting on some shelf of privacy that he must have learned to reach quickly and directly through long practice, travelling and performing as hard as he did, had done for thirty years.

Famous beyond famous, the ultimate show business machine, when you met him you could look and stare and still not really see him. Your real life was just another medium that he was starring in. But while he slept and I watched, something began happening to his face. The laughing aggression dissolved first into gentleness and then into a melting tenderness. Even the skin tone changed, and his face filled with what I could only call longing, although what he could still be longing for after his attainments, I don't know.

If you saw him in a sketch wearing a dress and wig and heels, you'd never think for a moment that you were looking at a woman, but he looked very feminine now. (Raquel Welch was sitting two seats away, providing a strong point of reference.) He cocked his head as though he was straining to hear something that was just a little too far away, and his hands began to move slowly, drifting back and forth like a soft-shoe dancer's hands. His smile grew even sweeter. I couldn't recall the leer that I thought had always been his only smile.

He was a wonderful dancer anyway, always underrated there. He expressed things in his dancing that were repressed and even strangled in his comedy, and even though he was only moving his hands now, the motion was so beautiful and soothing that I couldn't stop looking. I felt that I should but I couldn't, while years and layers of cover came away from him and there was nothing left in the icon face that I recognized. Except that I knew it was him. The name-in-the-face was still intact.

A few minutes later the helicopter started its descent and one of his people leaned across and touched his shoulder. His hands stopped. Looking at them now, I could believe that he had boxed with them. He opened his eyes and saw me. He was like a man snapping shut a secret album because someone had just come into the room. His features lengthened and sharpened, the old werewolf effect, he was already running through the lines he would be speaking in a few minutes, the lines that disgusted me that day and make me laugh now, and seem so touching.

> *"Well, here we are in Bien Hoa. Bien Hoa . . . that's Vietnamese for "Duck!" But say, what a reception I got at the airport. They thought I was a replacement . . ."*

I was back dissociating again, much better in wartime. The old soft-shoe man was out, re-possessed by Bob Hope, and in those few seconds I lost all interest in him.

Yankee Doodle. 1986

BING CROSBY

Call Me Lucky

"My name is being prominently featured in the newspapers and in the broadcasts, and considerable invaluable publicity thus redounds to me," the young jazz singer wrote to his mother in 1929, while he was touring with the Paul Whiteman Orchestra. He'd had a year or so of law at Gonzaga University, which might account for the diction. Not much of what he learned was ever wasted; the jazz he sang in those days, before there were any crooners, would show up in his music for the rest of his life. On the road, he roomed for a while with Bix Biederbeck, who almost never slept. Bix was so restless that he would wake Bing up in the middle of the night to change beds with him.

◆

Happy-go-lucky. Most people said that he just had no ambition at all, kicking that gong, falling through the drum. Look how wrong people can be. Easy going, perhaps, since his sled was lighter and faster than anyone else's, because so many people had been thrown off it in its swift

Solo. 1986

smooth course. So dear to a hundred million hearts, and so familiar, they say that he was functionally friendless, that he didn't have that capacity, or even that concept. Associates, colleagues, cronies, children; but no one who really knew him.

◆

He missed so many performances that Whiteman let him go, and when he went solo, he kept on missing them. When he got his own network radio program in 1931, he missed the first two broadcasts. Union problems, it was reported, and when that didn't go over, a bad cold was offered, then nodes on the vocal chords, and, finally, too much night-clubbing. He made the third broadcast though, and the rest is show business history, which means that there must be footnotes: After that broadcast, back at the hotel, his brother-manager Everett was getting ready for bed when he noticed a piece of paper lying on the floor.

Ev,
Cancel all contracts. I gave it all I had, and it's no go.

Bing

RICHARD NIXON

It's a big country, with many and diverse interests. No one has ever been elected President of all the Americans. It's assumed that a little crisis is good for the soul, but some people aren't satisfied unless there's all kinds of crises going on at all levels all the time, and they recognized from the beginning that he was the man for their job.

Those of us who couldn't give him our votes have never denied him our energy, including the countless assholes in Massachusetts who with totally misplaced pride displayed bumper stickers denying any responsibility for what we had all created together, The Crisis Man; that breathtakingly transparent front man up there disturbing the ghost of Harry Truman, working tirelessly and so successfully to finally and permanently de-mystify the Office, something that not even Warren Harding was able to accomplish. We knew everything he cared to tell us about the first six crises, and the six that would inevitably follow, and all the other connective crises, but no one will ever know the primary one, the ongoing inescapable crisis of actually having to be Richard Nixon.

◆

He wasn't the first drinker in the White House, and certainly not the first crook. But the pills gave the drinking an unusual complexion, and he was no ordinary crook either, because he had found the way to keep himself pathologically incapable of wrongdoing, abidingly unimpeach-

Steps. 1986

able. But we knew him anyway; much astonishment, no surprise. It didn't matter then, it doesn't matter now. In the smoky back room of the trick Republic, he will always be the favorite.

Instead of well-loved, he was well-connected. He was the born caretaker of other men's juices. He filled up with the juice that ran along the West Coast into the Pan-American artery, and down the East Coast to the tip of Florida, where it whipped across the Keys like ball lightning, once into Cuba, now into Haiti and the Bahamas; all the Gulf and offshore juices, and the juice that came up out of the Nevada Desert in gushers; from the Summa Corporation, Resorts International and the varied various Brotherhoods, international and local but never, alas, internal, for he was not a happy man, as anyone could plainly see. Which is probably why he always played the lighter emotions so broadly. (Although, come to think of it, his playing could go out of control in many directions at once.) In the whole history of the business, no act ever had a stronger finish. The bathos, the pathos, the laughter and tears, our dear dark star going off again into orbit.

◆

Human-all-too-human, Ecce Homo; as ambiguous as the Sphinx with too many riddles to even think about, the Winnerloser or the Loserwinner, which was which and what's the difference? Body speech and mind, his life has been a great lesson, given with complete generosity to the millions of us who can't stand the heat but don't know how to get out of the kitchen. And has anybody ever thanked him for that? No. Nor for the truly selfless way he went about binding up the Nation's wounds with the gauze and glue of his rhetoric, his incomparable rhetoric.

He used the language of democratic politics as a kind of degraded compost; always kept a big mound of it steaming nearby, wherever he stood, to establish a scale and to draw the flies of his selfhatred around him in droves. He hadn't personally, single-handedly degraded that language; nobody's accusing him of that, maybe the foulest of crimes. But he institutionalized that degradation, pushing himself forward like that all the time, with the flag in front of him, protecting him, always pushing and pushing with that flag, until the flag itself caught a puff of wind, and on the impulse drove him back.

EVEL KNIEVEL

"Ice water in a tight place," they sure did get it right when they named you.

No one's going to tell you not to do it, Evel, and nobody's going to be looking the other way when you're doing it, either. You said you could do it, you said you *would* do it, so you better just get out there now, pucker down and do it, do it for us one more time like a goddamned fool, go ahead and break your goddamned neck.

One Day King. 1979

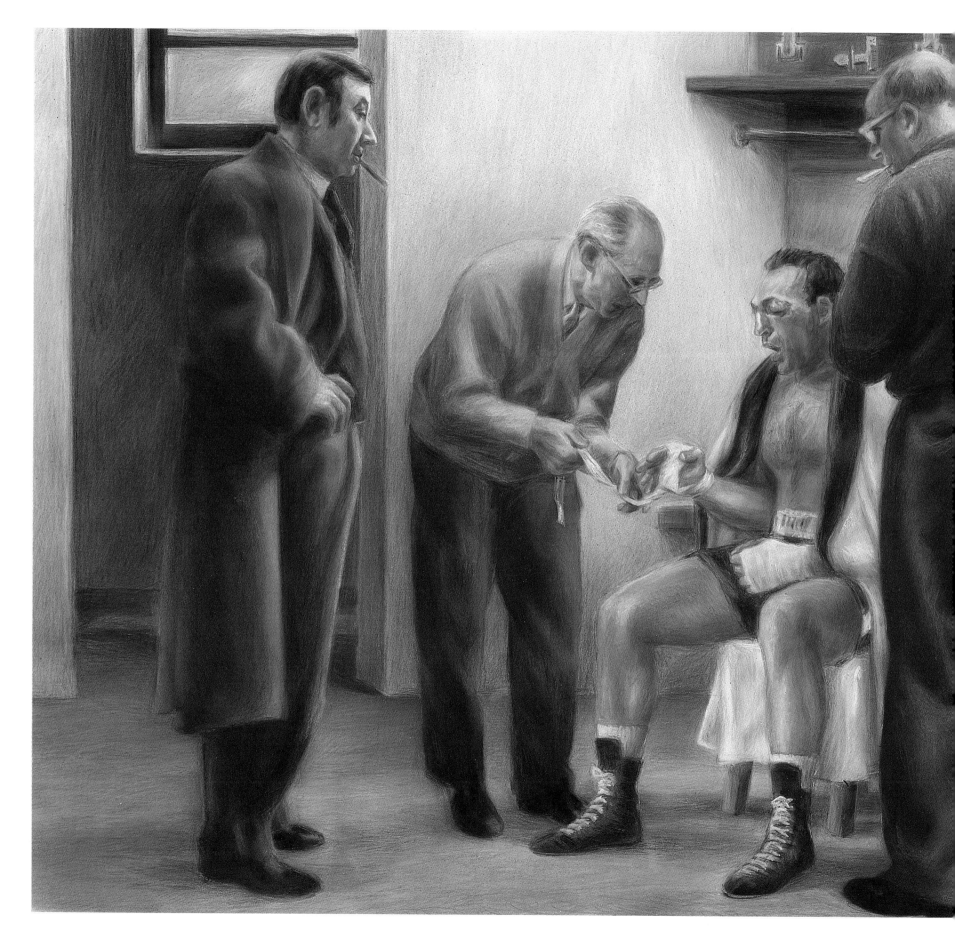

The Interview. 1986

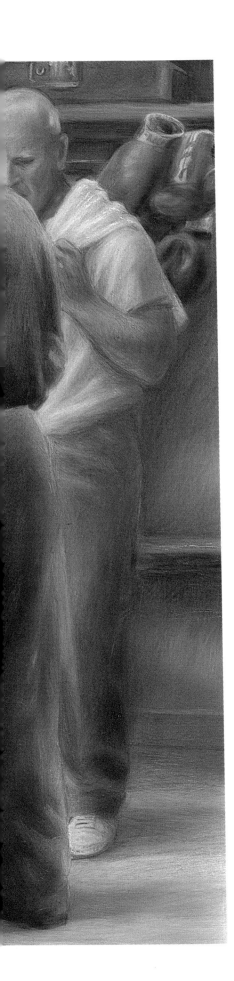

HOWARD COSELL

It's a long story, God is it a long story, how this smart Jew lawyer found his way deep into the hearts of so many ornery goys, often by bad-mouthing their heroes, drawing attention particularly to their brute greed and stupidity, but it's a story that only Howard should tell. (Just ask him.) It's enough, plenty, to say, as they used to say every Monday up in the booth and down in the lockers, "It isn't whether you win or lose, it's how you talk the game".

JOE NAMATH

Show Business and Sports had been cutting around together for years before Joe Namath got down on what was left of his knees and said, not in a shy way, "What the hell, we might as well get married."

This wasn't Bob Mathias for Wheaties anymore, building sharper reflexes for more and better morals. This was a display of how that old athletic piety had evolved since muscular Christianity was first diverted through the marketplace. Immodest maybe, but hardly immoral, and the fans went wild. "Go for it Joe Willie," they

Broadway Joe. 1985

cheered. "Go for the whole thing." His response, more than anything else, made him a hero.

He could go all night and have plenty left over for the game, do the Monkey *and* throw the long bomb, while maintaining sensational grace-to-pressure ratios. He played like a boy and walked like a man, he was the boy-man's boy-man. In those days, all the studs who weren't trying to be like Steve McQueen were trying to be like Joe Namath.

"He's single and young and doesn't have to be at work until noon," the Coach said. "You can't ask a man like that to sit at home and read a book."

ANN-MARGRET

Scoobie: A teenage "aloha", one word with a hundred meanings. Ann-Margret called her car, her bike, her dog, her friends and even herself Scoobie.

She longed for a strong man who would come and take over her life. Once in an interview she went so far as to lament that there were no Harry Cohns or Louis B. Mayers around anymore to tell her what to wear, how to do her hair, who to date.

"She makes you wonder whether to give her a stick of gum or a bracelet," one of her directors said. Presumably, he meant this as a compliment, a description of her mysterious quality at a time when a lot of people claimed that she didn't have any quality at all, only her twitch-pout-snarl and bump routine, kitten with a whip, a plaything for the New Frontier, to fool around with and forget.

Maybe the studio bosses weren't as tough as Harry Cohn, but they were strong enough to fashion a leash for her and keep it tight. Tribal Hollywood behavior, carnal speculation passing for knowledge, come across or take a walk. If she wouldn't arouse lust anymore, let her arouse laughter. Poor Scoobie.

She'd worked hard since she was four years old, with a child's innocent unobstructed dream of becoming a great entertainer loved by millions, and this was turning into a nightmare. She was outnumbered, surrounded and cut off. The last anyone saw of her, she was going in the wrong direction down some dirt road on the back of a bike with her legs wrapped around Joe Namath.

The kitten was totalled, but not the whip. The woman who walked away from the wreckage had it in her hand, and when she brought it down it cut the line where songs of innocence leave off and songs of experience begin.

The Choice. 1985

J.F.K.

The greatest of the historic Summit Meetings was being held at the Sands Hotel in late 1959. Frank's name was on the marquee outside, but the stage was so crowded those nights you could hardly tell whose engagement it was, or where the stage ended and the audience began. The whole Clan was there. They worked on their movie during the day and then did two shows every night. There were names everywhere you looked. They came down from the stage to sit at the tables, while others ran up to replace them, taking their drinks with them. Frank was in the middle of a ballad when Dean came weaving across the stage pretending to be loaded. Sammy jumped up doing his Jerry Lewis voice, "Dean, Dean, I made a boo boo," and they all broke up. Joey Bishop stood off to one side and heckled, while Berle and Rickles schpritzed them from ringside. Lawford was completely deadpan, looking on in mock disbelief at this madness. Nothing would make him crack until Sammy came flying on, tapdancing and snapping an imaginary rag. He made like he was shining Frank's shoes, and Lawford broke up too. The audience screamed, even when the gags were so inside that they didn't get them. They say you could hear gusts of laughter outside blowing across Highway 91 as you drove by, and nobody laughed harder or seemed to be having a better time than Frank's friend and personal guest, the Senator.

◆

The apple didn't fall far from the tree. Made in the shade, he was the most successful of

Surroundings. 1985

his father's many successful enterprises, and by far the most attractive. Ever since he was a boy he'd liked his fun, and known where, when and how to have it, if not always who to have it with. Which didn't matter much. There's nothing more becoming in a serious man than a developed sense of play.

He loved his brief visits to Las Vegas, and not only because it was so far from his constituency. He was the most starstruck of stars, (that never changed, even when he became the most famous man in the world), and his Vegas friends arranged everything there for him, especially seeing to it that his privacy would be respected, and he was always happy there. (It's an interesting question, more than a footnote but less than a thesis: Did they make him feel at home there, or did he just feel that way?) True, half the people he met there thought that "Senator" was just his nickname, but that's one of the things he liked about it. The smart money saw right away that it would not only be possible to run a Catholic for President, but totally all right, so long as it was as obvious to everyone else as it was to them that he was not a dogmatic Catholic.

Everybody was immediately charmed by the graceful yet forceful yet diffident way he spoke, and by his smile, which could have meant anything, but certainly meant something. In the informality of the place he could unwind, relax, and mix business with pleasure in the easy earnest way of a sharp young head completely unashamedly on the make, making friends and probably promises that he wouldn't be able to keep for very long, at least not openly. Because even then his kid brother was around like a mongoose on Benzedrine, watching, keeping tabs and running the connections down to their root-ends, to see exactly who was friends with who, and who to play up, or down, or chop completely. The older brother's playground was the younger brother's nightmare. Still, the action was invigorating. It's possible that more of the New Frontier was inspired here at the Sands than back on the Massachusetts bedrock or looking dreaming out of the office window at the Jefferson Memorial.

◆

"Hey what the hey!" Frank said. Dean was carrying Sammy onstage in his arms.

"Hallo dere," Dean smirked. "Congratulations. The NAACP wants that you should have this beeyoodiful award…" He dropped Sammy at Frank's feet.

Frank picked him up and hugged him. "This is a very great honor," he said. "I'm gonna take him home with me … Say, what do you people *eat?*" The audience screamed.

It was almost impossible to book a room anywhere in Vegas, and to get into the Sands you need more money than juice, and plenty of both. The town had never seen anything like it before, and never would again. There would be steady commercial increases over the next fifteen years, but what's money? There would never be the hyperglamour of those weeks again. It was the Sun at Noonday by which all decline is measured.

Those of us who only read about it in the columns and the magazines were sorry we weren't there, more than sorry, envious. But it wasn't as bad for us as it was for the losers who actually came so close, who saw the show and then got the Rat Pack brush, Let's Lose Charley, and were left downstairs when the party moved from the stage to Frank's suite, where it went on all night.

The atmosphere was so charged that nobody could take it all in. The events of those evenings turned into vacant nostalgia almost as they were happening, people woke up the next day and remembered the night before as though it had been ten years ago. And the room was so full of stars and star impulses that they cancelled each other out, turning themselves into mere people and even the shadows of mere people, and out of those shadows stepped a minor, purely parochial celebrity, so young and dishy that instead of everybody looking at Cary Grant, everybody was looking at Jack Kennedy.

SAMMY DAVIS JR.

"Skin me, Brer Fox," sez Brer Rabbit, sezee, "snatch out my eyeballs, t'ar out my years by de roots, en cut off my legs," sezee, "but do please, Brer Fox, don't fling me in dat brierpatch ..."

Hahahahahahaha, you little meshugenah you, tummel tummel tummel, you break me up. Nobody sings *My Way* more ways than Sammy, and I really mean that. You are the greatest black Puerto Rican Jewish one-eyed entertainer in the business – no, in the whole *history* of the business. Am I right, ladies and gentlemen, or am I right?

Co'se Brer Fox wanter hurt Brer Rabbit bad ez he kin, so he cotch 'im by de behime legs en slung 'im right in de middle er de brierpatch ...

So Sammy, tell these good people where you're working, I know they're all going to want to come out and see you. Well, maybe not *all*, let's face it, you seem to have two kinds of fans. The first really loves you and will go to see you. The others would prefer to stay home and receive you as a "found" act on the box because, after thirty years as a headliner and almost fifty in the business, you are obviously a survivor, and one of the things you've had to survive is their aversion to who they think you are, and to what you do. They just can't see past the *shtuck*, the gold embroidered dashikis, the love beads, platinum peace symbols, more tchotchkies than Sophie

Into the Circle. 1984

Tucker and twice as sentimental; drenched in humility dancing before kings and queens and presidents – maybe one president too many, a lot of people say, (while some of the brothers say, they can dig it that you danced for him, but did you have to *kiss* the motherfucker?)

But what are you going to do? That's show business, and I mean that sincerely, that *is* show business: they love you and they hate you, you're out there working, they can call you anything they feel like. I know you've often been seen as the token-totem, the little livery boy standing so perennial and patient holding the bridle-ring on the wide rolling front lawn of American Entertainment. But even that blatant medallion has another face, because somehow or other, you put yourself as far beyond the opposition's lines as anybody ever has, and so you stand for that, too, like a landmark. So Shalom, Bro. Familiarity like ours breeds something beyond contempt. Time-in counts for plenty, and we're more than used to you now, we're attached. The record shows, you took the blows, and did it your way.

"... *Bred en bawn in a brier-patch, Brer Fox – bred en bawn in a brier-patch!" En wid dat he skip out des es lively ez a cricket in de embers.*

BOBBY DARIN

"My, the boy comes on pretty strong," said Perry Como, the King of the Slow-mo, after working with Bobby Darin for the first time.

"I want to be a legend by the time I'm twenty-five," Bobby said, adding something rash about becoming bigger than Sinatra one day; to which Frank responded like a touchy but absolute *capo*, and never gave the boy a tumble. *Little Boy Brash, Angry Young Man of Show Business*, the fan magazines said. *What Makes Bobby Run?* And so forth.

"I want to make it faster than anyone ever made it before," he said, putting out the ring-a-ding-ding and the hup-hup-hup everywhere he went, to announce himself and to go out on, leaving behind live traces of aggression snapping in the air all over the business; up and down the unsettled border between the generations, between rock and roll and the Copa, and so swift that you couldn't tell whether he was a citizen of both ter-

Splish Splash. 1986

ritories, or of neither. He was having a "career" in the sense used to describe lava flow, or the course of hurricanes. (Like the career of another short, attack-prone Bobby, Darin's friend and political hero. In '68 they flew around together and sang duets in the back of the campaign plane, *Up a lazy river how happy we will be ...*) "I want to be in the upper echelons of show business to such an extent it's ridiculous." A nervy little cat for sure. I want I want I want.

◆

He was so frail and sickly as a baby that nobody expected him to live. According to him, the neighbors in the South Bronx tenement where he was a child used to tell his mother, "Whaddya wanna wheel that thing around for? It's gonna die!" (It must have been a very tough neighborhood indeed.) Growing up, he developed the refined but aggravated time sense people have when they know in their bodies how tenuous their engagement really is. There couldn't be anything tenuous about his career.

What made it so exciting, and endearing, was that he wasn't actually in such a hurry as he seemed. The push and speed were there just for the weight. His heart worked out of rhythm, rheumatic but accurate as the most delicate chronometer. It told him the time, and it told him the deal, and it was always the same. To us it looked like he was way ahead, but he knew he was running late. He could make it big and even big big and still keep running if he wanted to, but he could never catch up.

COLONEL PARKER / ELVIS PRESLEY

Do the chairs in your parlour,
Seem empty and bare?
Do you gaze at your doorway,
And picture me there?

Nobody said it for us better than the Colonel, or pierced the problem more cleanly when the grief came pyramiding into Memphis from all around the world, and the flowers that followed could be weighed by the ton and measured in miles, but no method could be formulated to quantify the loss, and no words could be found to qualify it. It was reported then that his manager (mentor, exploiter, high or low chamberlain, whatever you want to call him, a business-show-man but a great rock and roller for all of that), brought his people together and made an oration of his own.

"Nothing has changed," he told them. "It's just like when my boy went into the Army."

Morning Sun. *1978*

Is your heart filled with pain?
Shall I come back again?
Tell me dear,
Are you lonesome tonight?

Pontypridd. 1977

TOM JONES

The singing hod-carrier, no one had ever made singing so resemble manual labor before. The Pride of Pontypridd, where as a boy he stood up on orange crates singing *Mule Train* in the high street for shillings, shaking his moneymaker until the shillings became dollars, millions of them, and instead of coins his fans threw their room keys at him. Perhaps it was his trousers, or the hernia-defying way he stood when he sang, offering himself, that excited his particular audience. And maybe it was his blatant business aspect, as though he was less a singer than a paid escort, with the songs included in the fee. Whatever it was, they certainly wanted it.

Tom, called Tiger Tom and Tom Terrific and Toreador Tom, highest paid matador in the history of the great Plaza de Toros de Las Vegas. Even Elvis came like a schoolboy to watch and learn, because no one had ever worked so close to the horns as Tom Jones. (Were the horns shaved? ¿Quien sabe?)

"You see," Tom explained, "kids don't really know why they're doing all that screaming, but a thirty-five-year-old woman has a better idea." And, by chrono/logical extension, a fifty-year-old woman would have an even better idea, fifteen years better, since if there's one thing we, or anyway Tom Jones, learned from the Sixties, it's that young ideas are not necessarily good ideas.

JOHNNY CARSON

"Mr. Carson, how did you become a star?"
"I started out in a gaseous state, and then I cooled."

At the intersection where television life, real life and dream life are supposed to cross, the heaviest traffic in the history of the world has accumulated. Nothing's moved through there for a long time. The lights have been broken for thirty years, and now they can't be fixed. In the critical midnight hour, someone's got to stand there and look like he's keeping the congestion down. It's not a thankless job, it's just hopeless. It broke a lot of men before Johnny Carson came along, and a lot since, and some of them were good men too, or at least all right.

You know the drill: It's late at night, you're lying there with the TV on and your thoughts in their untamed abundance and variety, your rising dread and snowballing expectations, your speculations, your splinter of interest floating on a sea of distraction, your wants and don't-wants, likes and dislikes, hopes, fears, etc., with the one you love by your side or maybe not, and Johnny Carson.

One viewer was reminded of Jay Gatsby, because of the remoteness as well as a certain virgin American beauty, a man totally in charge but vulnerable, way over there and full of secrets. Actually, this viewer was seeing him not on television but at a party in Beverly Hills. She was an un-named and convenient starlet, quoted by Kenneth Tynan in his profile of Carson, and though I suspect him of new journalism here, there's nothing suspect about the comparison.

There's probably never been another comic with Johnny Carson's range, slow if he wants to be, fast when he has to be, like a machine but not a machine. He'll play it broad but seldom low, and never loud. What you hear in the space between jokes is a purring sound, and whatever it may be doing to your mind, there's nothing the matter with his mind. He knows. What Milton Berle took on in all innocence in the frontier days, Johnny Carson has taken on in knowledge.

Whether he's a master of the art of conversation or not, he's certainly a master of talking to people on television, and come to think of it, what fool ever said that conversation is an art anyway? Master of many show business forms, master of the late night ceremony, a breeze in the claustrophobia, dispatcher of the national consciousness from waking into sleep, smooth as an airwave, tele-reflexive. And yet the word on him is that he's a little cold. Well, you'd go cold too, sitting in that chair, between Cathode and Psyche. It makes me feel cold just thinking about it. They'd have to pay me a lot of money to do that job. Here's Johnny.

Room with TV. 1986

MUHAMMAD ALI

The Half-Dream Room

A heavy blow takes you to the door of this room. It opens, and you see neon, orange and green lights blinking ... Weird masks and actor's clothes hang on the wall.

The first time the blow sends you there, you panic and run, but when you wake up you say, "Well, since it was only a dream, why didn't I play it cool, put on the actor's clothes, the mask, and see what it's like?" Only you have to do it in your mind and plan to do it long before the half-dream comes. You have to put the plan in your mind long before you need it.

In the half-dream room time seems to stretch out slow, and unless you've been there before, you'll never know how fast it goes by.

— From *The Greatest, My Own Story*
by Muhammad Ali

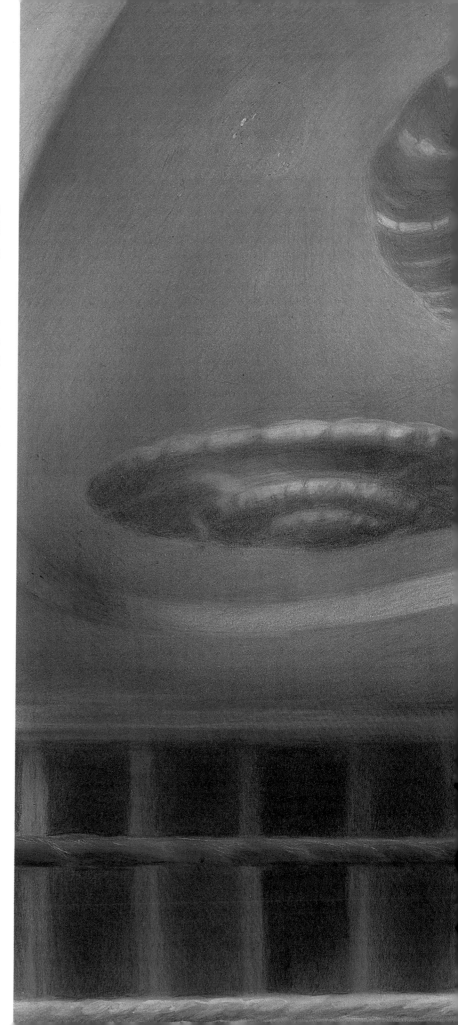

Caesar's Palace. 1985

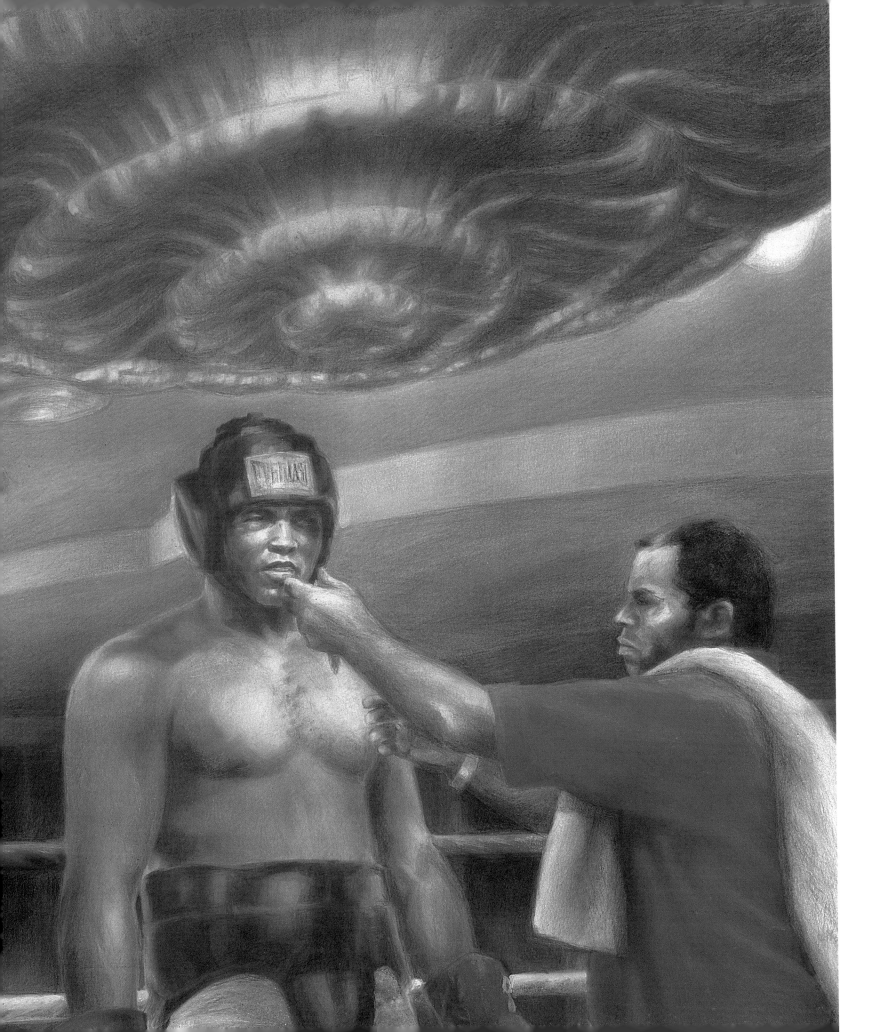

Elysée. 1985

ORSON WELLES

The Real Kenosha Kid

Hey presto, and a corny old abracadabra. What an ingenious and simple deception, an actual wizard goes out in the world disguised as a common vaudeville magician. Sleight of heavy hand to draw the willing eye away from the real mastery: tricks with shadows and light, handkerchiefs and crystal balls, voices coming out of empty boxes; whatever works; whatever diverts; beards, brogues, capes, shamelessly with mirrors. (The Great Orsoni even sawed a woman in half, but when he did the trick the woman was Marlene Dietrich.)

Just to hear that voice is to experience a richness that would otherwise have been beyond our means, emanating from that fabulous deep cavern, while the boy genius who has always lived inside the shadows there comes and goes as he pleases. Well, almost as he pleases, since being Orson Welles has often been a luxury that not even Orson Welles could afford.

◆

"What a pity there are so many of me, and so few of you," he told an audience; an apt and amusing Wellesian joke, with layers of intention from the most frivolous and self-appreciating to the most sombre, which only goes to show (as though we needed another demonstration), The Kenosha Kid can kid you, but you can't kid The Kenosha Kid.

MEYER LANSKY

I believe that here it is a question of cruelty used well or badly. We can say that cruelty is used well (if it is permissible to talk in this way of what is evil) when it is employed once for all, and one's safety depends on it, and then it is not persisted in but as far as possible turned to the good of one's subjects. Cruelty badly used is that which although infrequent to start with, as time goes on, rather than disappearing, grows in intensity. Those who use the first method can, with divine and human assistance, find some means of consolidating their position; the others cannot possibly stay in power.

— The Prince

Sh'mah Yisroel Adonai Eluhainu Adonai E'Chod, Hear oh Israel, the Lord our God the Lord is One. But here in the world that we can see and taste we have business, and once, every hundred years or so, someone with a mind like Meyer Lansky's to do the business. So much business, so thoroughly done, that a lot of superstitious people came to believe that Lansky had more juice than Jehovah. And since they all went down one after another and Meyer didn't, you couldn't totally blame them. Exciting such strong emotions in others, he seldom expressed emotions of his own. Instead, he formed a great organization to express them for him. Above it, always on top of it, he quietly indulged his two passions, one for the numbers, one for anonymity, and quietly he commanded respect from the men of respect, and fear, and absolute loyalty. For example:

> *So long as the blood flows in my body do I, Santo Trafficante, swear allegiance to the will of Meyer Lansky and the organization he represents. If I violate this oath, may I burn in hell forever.*

The above was transcribed, and then signed by Mr. Trafficante in his own blood, drawn with a dagger provided for the ceremony by Lansky, and witnessed by Lansky and an associate. They'd come all the way to Havana to get this business over with. As soon as Trafficante left the room, they laughed so hard they could barely stand up.

This was 1957, at the time that Lansky was lining up support against Albert Anastasia to maintain what had been his from the beginning, his because it began in his mind, control of the National Crime Syndicate. "You bastards have sold yourselves to the Jews!" Anastasia had shouted to his people in the boardroom; maybe, but not cheaply. That particular trial of Lansky's strength ended in a chair in the barbershop of the Park Sheraton Hotel, the same hotel where somebody had killed Arnold Rothstein almost thirty years before.

♦

He had a couple of war names when he was young: Johnny Eggs for some reason, and Bug (or one of the Bugs, since there was Moran in Chicago, and there was Meyer's teenage pal, protégé, partner in the Bug and Meyer Mob and spiritual kid brother, Ben Siegel, the one true Bug). Later, when people called him the Little Man, it would be in his absence and always as a term of respect, sometimes even of endearment (not that he cared), a spoken certificate of his position. But to his face, even before he was twenty-five years old, it was formal-style, Meyer to his friends, Mr. Lansky to everyone else.

In the old underworld, it was hard to lose a handle once you'd acquired one. Think of Scarface, Greasy Thumb, Kid Twist; Nig, Boob, Blinkie, Moonie and Longie; Lepke and Gurrah (aka The Gold Dust Twins), Farvel, Dutch, Legs, Ice-Pick, Bats, Socks, the Enforcer, the Stick, the Waiter, the Peasant, Trigger Mike, Sleep Out Louie, No Nose Tony, Three-Fingered Brown, Jimmy Blue Eyes: all figures associated with Lansky at one time or another, and mostly examples of the kind of flash hood he despised. They had no mentality. It wasn't enough that they controlled all the business in three boroughs, or

the South Side or the North Side, they wanted to be opera stars too. Maybe it was because as kids they'd grown up in the legend gap, the only one the country has ever had. The West was tame, settled and unheroic, and there weren't any movie stars yet, so they got the bad idea that they would be the heroes, with their colorful names and thrilling adventures, the Curbstone Rangers. But they had such filthy tempers, and unbearable vanity. Their pride stank, their secret society wasn't secret enough, and no matter what they said, they weren't really putting business first.

In the early Prohibition days, the Jewish gangsters were concentrated under Waxey Gordon and Arnold Rothstein, the Brain, who fixed the 1919 World Series and broke a nation's heart. The Irish bosses were Owney Madden and Big Bill Dwyer, while the Italians moved their commitments back and forth between Joe Masseria and Salvatore Maranzano, both fighting for the title in the wake of the last absolute boss, Ignazio Saietta, Lupo the Wolf, *capo di capi re*. Neighborhood gangs came up and went down, the Families ran their city states, blood related but divided by distance and interests, the blood anyway not even as thick as water, doing Rigoletto all over the streets anytime they felt like it, with lots of bystanders falling in the crossfire, children too. It drew civic heat and burned up profits, and what for?

Meyer Lansky clucked his tongue and shook his head at the waste. He kept still in the middle of the furious emotional games and practiced self-control, knowing even then that it was the only control worth anything. Being smart, and discreet, he naturally fell in with people who were also smart and discreet, and he told them, in so many words, "Listen, this is America. There's plenty. There's ways of getting along with everyone. It's not strictly true that you can't make somebody like you."

He started in using that kugel of his, and by the time he was finished a lot of Italians and Irish (and Chinese, Mexicans, Cubans, Colombians, Haitians, Dominicans, Swiss, Afro-Americans, quite a few Presbyterians and several Presidents, to say nothing of other Jews), were wondering if it wasn't true after all that Jews were smarter than everybody else.

♦

It was Johnny Torrio, the aptly named Fox, who told Lansky to read Machiavelli. Torrio said it would reveal the Italian mind to him. What Lansky found there instead was the italianate version of wisdom he already had, or would have soon; with a few exceptions, (Torrio, Costello, Luciano), the Italians he knew didn't have minds like that. Machiavelli said that a prince had to be conservative in peace and radical in war. A prince must choose a hero from history and always keep him in his thoughts. (Lansky was still a schoolboy when he chose Napoleon.) Punishment should be swift, "once for all", and benefits gradual; a prince must build a militia. (Not being one of the "made guys" himself, he didn't carry a gun, but under his command, and only his command, never to be used except by him or with his permission, were standing companies of soldiers; buttonmen, goons and blades, with Goolyas for Gurkhas; good fighters, silent and irrecoverable as torpedoes once you sent them out.) He read how to control Pistoia (or New York, or Detroit) by faction, and Pisa (or L.A., Miami, Havana, Hot Springs, Biloxi, Port-au-Prince, one day Las Vegas) by fortress; and under which circumstances good deeds can become bad enemies, e.g., "Whenever that class of men on which you believe your continued rule depends is corrupt, whether it be the populace, the soldiers, or the nobles."

♦

In 1932, Lansky and Luciano came to Chicago to attend the Democratic Convention, along with Ben Siegel and Frank Costello. They were there as infra-delegates, strictly unofficial. They held talks with Curley of Massachusetts, Pendergast of Kansas, Huey Long of Louisiana, and Jimmy Hines of New York City and Tammany Hall. Through Hines, they delivered the New York City vote which Roosevelt needed to win the nomination. And as soon as he became President, Roosevelt turned and smashed all their machines. That impressed Lansky, and suited him, cutting out (as he thought it would) the greedy middlemen who stood between elected officials and what Roosevelt called "the Underworld-lings".

It was an inspiring time. Big government was reaching out to industry and business with a new set of codes, and however the company law-yers decoded them, they meant enforced partner-ship. Big invisible government could do the same, would have to, now that Repeal was coming.

After more than ten years of planning, the National Crime Syndicate was finally formed in 1934, under the leadership of Lansky and Lu-ciano. Many of its ideas came directly from the Roosevelt Administration. It was a new deal, a National Recovery Act of Crime, terribly hard on the old Moustaches but perfect for young, am-bitious hyphenated Americans who weren't a-fraid of a little hard work and a few risks. It imme-diately established regional boards, a system of audits and a high commission that could settle disputes with a gesture or a phone call, the ulti-mate in binding arbitration. Like the daring new government in Washington, the NCS was im-placably centrist, committed to diversified own-ership while remaining as far as you could get from being enemies of Capitalism. And they were

6 a.m., Collins Ave. 1985

streamlined. What it took Roosevelt a hundred days to just barely establish, Lansky and Luciano already had established, almost overnight, with the precedent of the Sicilian Vespers. If they wanted to pack their supreme court, who had the moxie to reverse them? And anyway, it was constitutional. It wasn't our thing or their thing or anybody's thing anymore. It was a corporation, with corporate rules and policies, and over it a living corporation watchword; *Cui Bono*, Who Benefits?

◆

Lansky's reach never exceeded his grasp. His style was so classic and simple that it was beautiful (if it is possible to talk in this way of what is evil): Run a line into the prospective enterprise as quietly as possible, even if it takes years longer that way. Nurture the line, which means nurture the people all along the line, cutting away whatever refuses nourishment. Attach one end securely and then, without ever touching it personally, never let go of the other end. Never, unless it overheats or barring an act of God, or a revolution. In other words, attach the line to you, not vice-versa. During his lifetime, the boundary between the rackets and legitimate business became so pale and shadowy as to be almost imaginary. The concept of "crime" became as archaic as "government for the people", until hardly a man, woman or child in the whole country could go through a single day without eating his wafer at least once, and making communion with him, a man they never even heard of, so they never knew who to thank. And that's how smooth it ran under Meyer Lansky.

There's a load of lox and bagel
For a cowboy in Las Vegal.

— Mule Train (Mickey Katz version)

According to Lansky's biographer, Hank Messick, the sixteen-year-old Lansky was on his way from the tool-and-die factory where he worked, when he heard a woman's screams and shouting in Italian coming from the ground floor of an abandoned house. He went in to investigate. He found a twelve-year-old boy lying on the floor with his pants down and his cock sticking up, an hysterical teenage girl, and a dark twenty-one year old man who was kicking the girl across the floor. The twelve-year-old came up suddenly with a knife, and Lansky, to stop things from getting worse, took a small crowbar from his toolbox, made a couple of fast calculations, and knocked the older man unconsious. The boy with the knife was Ben Siegel and the young man was Salvatore Lucania, soon to be called Charles Luciano, then Lucky Luciano, and Charley Lucky.

It's hard to know how to accept this story of three-way love-at-first-sight, meeting violent but cute on the sidewalks of New York, 1918. Except of course for Lansky's initial careless interference, the behavior of the principals in this scene is consistent with their subsequent histories: the mad dog as a snapping puppy, the severe and methodical peacekeeper, and the hot-blooded Sicilian right from Central Casting, who was nevertheless cool enough and smart enough to know when he had been done a favor. (As for the girl, with whom Bugsy had been trying to lose his virginity, he saw her eight years later in a bar. She had gotten fat and drink had aged her badly, but he followed her out anyway, and raped her.)

◆

Twenty-five years passed, and many things hadn't changed. Luciano, monitoring the action carefully from his exile in Sicily, said that Siegel's balls were still bigger than his brains. Lansky knew better than Lucky, but he loved Siegel more than Lucky did. Maybe it was a weakness, the soft spot.

When Siegel went out West for the first time, to take over the racing wire on the Coast, it must have been Lansky's idea. And the whole tsimmis with Las Vegas must have been with Lansky's okay, which is to say, his protection. (Which is also to say, with Luciano's protection, since the two men always voted alike.) Maybe Lansky believed in Siegel's plan to turn Vegas into the greatest gambling-resort town in the world. Maybe it was remote enough to make a suitable outpost of progress. Maybe he persuaded his associates that men who spent as much time in hotels as they did ought to own a few themselves. But Meyer was behind it, definitely. There could have been no other way for Siegel to obtain two million Syndicate dollars just to start with and then run it up to six million, while remaining provocatively unaccountable to the Syndicate for a penny of it, as though it was nobody's business but his. This was Meyer Lansky's Gethsemane, three times bad; bad for business, bad for relations, bad for the Jews.

"Kill him," the board of the Nevada Projects Corporation voted. ("Farlo fuori", actually), with only the Lansky bloc against. The last reprieve was a formality and was granted, not for old times' sake, but because it was covered by Lansky's word. For the disaffected Directors, the short delay could only sweeten the outcome.

But Siegel was lost to headquarters. Meyer didn't have the vigorish there anymore, Virginia Hill had it. That *nafke*; the Flamingo Hotel was the Taj Mahal Bugsy was building to their painful obsessive love, even though the place gave her the creeps. She hated the desert so much that she developed an allergic reaction to it.

"They're like children," Meyer said. He'd seen Benny chasing the women for twenty-five years, but never one woman so single-mindedly. It surprised him and then it concerned him. He believed that Virginia brought out the worst in Siegel, and the worst of that was, she was smart. And careful. The word on her was that she had more underworld stories written down than Damon Runyon, locked away in safe deposit in the event of her violent death. Meyer must have respected her for that, and hated her.

When Bugsy and Virginia slipped away to Mexico and were married secretly, it must have been because they didn't want Lansky to know. Fat chance. He had eyes in Mexico. And anyway, where Siegel was concerned, what didn't he know? The last time they met (at the Flamingo, where Meyer was never seen to leave his room), they quarreled bitterly. Lansky told Siegel to calm himself down, arranged to meet with him in a few days in L.A., and they parted, Bugsy to finish his brief run, and Lansky to return to his meditations.

◆

The American tanks that came ashore on Sicily in 1944 flew bright yellow flags, each with a large L, as a signal to the waiting and extremely well organized partisans that the full invasion had begun. The L of course was for Luciano, but it could just as well have been for Little Man, since he had been one of the operation's main co-ordinators, standing patiently in the chain of diminishing respectability that ran between Roosevelt in command and Luciano in the old country.

As we've seen, Roosevelt had good reason to know that Meyer Lansky was a man to be trusted completely in sensitive negotiations. The year before, using Naval Intelligence as the broker, he had sent Lansky to Havana to obtain assurances from Presidente Fulgencio Batista that the coming Cuban elections would be free and open. Roosevelt had suggested using the U.S. Fleet as stick, but Lansky shrugged off such unwieldy and uneconomic means of enforcement. He got what he wanted simply, by holding talks with Batista, his friend and partner, indicating to him the many compensations he would receive for the loss of his office. And in the early months of the war, he and Luciano had worked to straighten out the labor problems threatening to close the vital New York–New Jersey docks.

For these and probably other services to his adoptive country, Meyer Lansky was rewarded with sanctions that protected and extended his privacy. He may even have received immunity from Federal prosecution. (His one conviction, in 1952, was on gambling charges, non-Federal, ninety days.) As far as J. Edgar Hoover was always claiming to be concerned, organized crime in America was the province of something called The Mafia. There was not nor could there ever be any such thing as a man named Meyer Lansky belonging to The Mafia.

May the words of my mouth, and the meditations of my heart, be acceptable oh Lord in Thy Sight … Who wants to read another book of gangster memoirs, so shabby and vindictive, so self-serving, crude and cowardly, with every page proceeding from the obvious premise of complete betrayal, broken oaths, unmanly kiss and tell? Unless of course they were *his* memoirs. Imagine that one, the Meyer Papers; an Education, a clarification, an absolute Torah of American practical conduct. What a book. And what a laugh, to even dream that the material for such a book would ever have been found among his papers. He never used a fountain pen to rob anyone in his life, he certainly wouldn't use one to amuse, or to tell what is nobody's affair. People know too much already, or think they do. It only makes them unhappy, schmoozling around where it doesn't concern them, and besides, (as he might have added), are you absolutely sure you want to know, "How's business Meyer?"

He kept it in his head. All the things we most want to know would be exactly the things he would never write down, never tell to more than one other living soul. All in his head, and not just names, dates and numbers, but the thing itself, the line he ran beneath our bottom line so he could catch whatever fell through the cracks, the whole underequation of American life. For shame, all the gossip, the confidences taken so lightly (Cui Bono?); knowledge is power but silence is knowledge, force is natural to beasts and law to men *So a prince must understand how to make a nice use of the beast and the man.* Business is good, and very long.

In the face of the sheerest mortality, but not by accident, he outlived almost everyone; his few friends, his many associates, certainly his rivals. Bugsy and Virginia, (chronic and clinical suicides); Torrio, Lucky, Costello, Genovese, Anastasia, (cancer, stroke and the bullet) and the Little Man became the little old man, enjoying the fruits of his thought, with a new generation in place and operating, ending his days on Miami Beach in his ingenious disguise, the consummate incognito. You could see him every morning at dawn (at that age they don't need much sleep), a grandfather among the grandfathers, an old cocker who made it when you could keep it, another semi-retired businessman, a little old Jewish man in a business suit walking his dog on Collins Avenue.

The Portrait. 1984

FRANK SINATRA

*"How did all these people
get in my room?"*

All or Nothing at All

The letterpaper was covered with lipstick kisses. "I love you so much it hurts," she wrote. "Do you think I should see a doctor?"

The quantum leap in Sensation, new levels of pressure in seven million teenage bedrooms. Tender blue eyes that he closed when he sang. That voice, those bones.

*H, and a U, and a B, B, A
Hubba Hubba Frankie Hey*

"Fainting, which once was so prevalent, had become a lost art among the ladies," the President said to him. "I'm glad you have revived it." They were having tea one afternoon in 1944. Later, as he was leaving the White House, Sinatra told reporters, "I felt as though I'd seen a vision. I thought, there is the greatest guy alive today and here's a little guy from Hoboken shaking his hand." That's what he felt, thought, and said; but what did he see?

The House I Live In

It wasn't the greatest part of town, but it wasn't Dead End either. Whatever it really was or wasn't, his mother was a powerful figure there, wardheeling for the Democrats, brokering the votes and favors, administering if not controlling the patronage in the lower middle-class largely Italian neighborhood where the families had so many children they didn't know what to do.

Francis Albert was an only child. He weighed 13 1/2 pounds at birth. The forceps scarred his head and face, and he wasn't breathing. As he turned blue and they stood there crossing themselves, somebody grabbed him and plunged him into cold water.

In the early Prohibition days when he was growing up, it's not hard to imagine who wrote the arrangements and led the band from the Hoboken Docks to City Hall, and how rough things could get. The violence of those streets may never have touched his actual person as often or severely as he would later claim, but it certainly must have entered his mind, inspiring him to re-invent his childhood and to say that if he hadn't become a singer, he'd have probably become a gangster. (Ethnic hyphenated feudal America, steeping and burning in the melting pot but not melting. And chief among the virtues is Loyalty, whose other face is Revenge. Who made this code? Why is it so familiar? What's the problem?)

Full Moon and Empty Arms

"It was the war years, and there was a great loneliness."

When he first went solo and Benny Goodman introduced him on the stage of the Paramount Theatre, the sound that came up from the audience stunned him. Goodman had been in front of wild crowds many times, but this was a sound that no one had ever heard before. It froze Sinatra in the wings, and if Goodman hadn't blurted out "What the hell was *that?*" so spontaneously, he never could have come on and sung, realizing immediately that he had really made that sound himself, even though it was coming from them; from their hearts and stomachs and the place that many of them didn't even have a name for, or at least one that they could say. From their you-knows, their down-theres.

"There's this one girl who's always in the audience. When I look accidentally in her direction, she lets out an awful yell. And sometimes she gets hysterical. The other morning she got that way and they told her they'd let her come up and see me. When I saw her, she was still crying. After a while she promised she'd be good if I'd give her my bowtie. So I did and she promised to be quiet. The next day, I got out on the stage and there she was yelling worse than ever."

Let Us Wander By the Bay

*"I understand the distance
necessary per phrase."*

A thin nearly wasted looking young man sits for hours at the piano, in empty theatres and rehearsal halls, late at night and early in the morning, playing scales and singing the same phrase over and over until everybody else has been driven away. *Let us wander by the bay*, Frank Sinatra's Rosebud. Nobody knows where the phrase comes from or what it means to him. When he was eighteen, touring with the Hoboken Four, he sat up all night in the back of the bus singing to himself. They'd yell at him to shut up so they could sleep, but he wouldn't. Two of his partners in the act used to smack him around all the time, for his stubbornness, and because he got all the attention in performance, and all the women. One day he said to the third member of the quartet, "Why don't you beat me too and make it unanimous?"

He listened to everything: To opera for its emotional license, to Billie Holiday for nuance and registration of pain, even in the uptempo. He followed the motion of Heifetz's bow over the strings for the measure that gave melody a "warm flowing unbroken quality". Later, he watched and studied Tommy Dorsey for a year, trying to learn the secret of his impossibly long lines, until he found the pinprick airhole in the corner of Dorsey's mouth. So incredibly simple, so useful.

He sang for carfare and cigarette money. He did three local broadcasts in Jersey every day, six days a week, at dawn, noon and midnight. He worked cellars and roadhouses and clubs where he doubled as vocalist/headwaiter. Anyplace, anyhow, for the singing itself and the exposure, until Harry James heard him and hired him, and even then he didn't let up.

He ran every day to build up his breath. He would swim the length of Olympic-size pools underwater, singing the lyrics in his head until he could cover six bars without breaking, which beat everybody else around by at least two bars. And, while he was down there, he worked out the code by which the completeness of romantic love would be expressed in popular music well into the rock and roll era; to this day in fact.

People used to laugh when they first looked at him, but after they heard him sing they didn't see him the same way again. Those were in the days before white pop records had a sound in the sense that movies had a look that expressed more of the story than the script. Other singers knew right away that he was singing from another place, as Billie Holiday would tell the cats who were always putting him down, on account of the bobbysox thing.

I Could Write a Book

"That night the bus pulled out with the rest of the boys at about half-past midnight. I'd said good-bye to them all and it was snowing I remember. There was nobody around and I stood alone with my suitcase in the snow and watched the tail-lights disappear. Then the tears started and I tried to run after the bus."

His ten months with the Harry James Orchestra was the happiest time of his life, he always said afterward. Happy, and safe. He went from a local to a minor national celebrity, and then Tommy Dorsey offered him a job with his much more popular band. It was the break that he'd worked so hard for, and James knew it. He let him out of their contract with a handshake and best wishes, and the bus pulled out, leaving Sinatra alone on the last threshold before the fame beyond fame.

Later, when he left Dorsey, the contractuals weren't so amicable. One story says that the price was one dollar, paid to the Sentimental Gentleman of Swing by Willie Moretti of New Jersey, in what has become the legendary if not completely mythical "offer you can't refuse". The papers supposedly still exist that document the release-fee and percentage story, but the Moretti story is the one everyone likes to believe, so maybe it's true, maybe not. Either way, we'll never know what really happened until we read Frank Sinatra's memoirs.

Speak Low

"I stepped off the plane in Havana with a small bag in which I carried my oils, sketching materials and personal jewelry, which I never send with my regular luggage."

Stepping with him from the plane, and clearly on friendly terms, were the Fischetti Brothers from Chicago, who had changed their reservations to fly with Sinatra when they heard that he was making the trip. Lucky Luciano was in town all that month, having somehow slipped away from his exile in Sicily to hold business meetings at the Hotel Nacional with a number of important visitors from the States. The papers tried to assert that, along with his cufflinks and charcoal, Sinatra was carrying two million dollars in cash as a favor to some people who couldn't make the trip themselves, but that's unlikely. It would have taken more luggage than Sinatra was carrying to hold that much money. It is true that Sinatra and Luciano met several times that week, but what could he have done? If you're with a bunch of people and you find yourself at a dinner-table with a guy, you don't just get up and walk away like a slob.

And while we're at it, if some guy from the rackets gets up at a party and sings "I'll Be Seeing

You", nobody calls him a reputed singer. If he does it all the time, the worst he'd be called is a dilettante, a pest. If he goes to the clubs or even the dressing rooms, nobody calls him a habitual associate of entertainers. Or is this just an attempt to force some perspective? A few days before Luciano died, the police searched his home in Italy and found a gold cigarette case, inscribed, "To Charlie, From His Pal, Frank Sinatra". Hardly anybody believes that they were really "pals".

◆

(*The House I Live In*, Take 2: Always room for the little man, no toleration for the abuses of power, open and light with good ventilation, and pictures of the President in every room, but which President? Frank Sinatra's not talking; how are we going to make up our minds if we don't have the facts? We could always do what his actual pal Jack Kennedy was forced to do later, and place him under "quiet investigation", to see if he might prove an embarrassment to us, or even whether we can still be embarrassed.)

Without a Song

> "*I got a broken mirror in my throat . . .*
> *It's cold up here . . .*"

The higher the top the longer the drop, hey Frank? (No heroes without adversity.)

Now, it seems the most compelling chapter of the legend, because until then the legend only had one layer to it. It began sometime around 1948, the lonely public death of Frank Sinatra, made even more excruciating by an international supporting cast of starlets, producers, bullfighters, hoods, columnists, headwaiters and photographers. *Assassinos*, hornets around his head, stardust in the Vaseline.

By 1950, he had the drawing power of an accident victim in the street. He was lucky to get a booking, and then lucky to draw two hundred people, most of whom heard his changing style as proof of his decline. He played the Paramount to empty balconies. His record company dropped him, and then his agents, for whom he'd made millions. He was on a roll of unreturned phone calls and averted glances. Most of his show business friends avoided him, even the ones he'd been nice to on the way up. He stood still then for the skinny-guinea jokes, and took it while they did everything to humiliate him but dress him up in donkey ears. *Gaffone*, and probably worse, *cornuto*, and it didn't look like he was doing it his way at all.

Everything Happens to Me

"He gave me a look. I can't describe it. I followed him out. I hit him. I'm all mixed-up."

Stuck-up little hotshot, him and his privacy. A lot of newspaper people had been waiting a long time for this, particularly the Hearst papers, who had always seen this (lefty) upstart (dago) as a threat to their (interests) morality. His singing was little better than degenerate jazz for white teenage men and women who could be embracing higher idols and ideals than Frankie (swoon), or that man in the White House.

What a coincidence, his power base shrivelling away like that at the very moment he needed to feel most like a man and have his manhood most under his control, for the massive passion that was playing itself out in hotel suites, nightclubs, airports and movie locations in L.A., New York, Madrid and Nairobi. Just when he could least afford a reckless move, he did what he'd sung about so many times but never really done. He found a good hot fire, and jumped into it.

In retrospect, the most dramatic aspect of that famous love affair with Ava Gardner was the cruelty it drew out of the press and the public in Chaplin-hating, Ingrid Bergman-baiting 1950 America. The most faithful of his fans were also the most sentimental. They had invested far too much in the fairytale of his marriage to Nancy, even though they might have known better. When he went public and wild with Ava, he lost them overnight, and then behaved as though it was good riddance. His pals tried to restrain him (including Willie Moretti, who sent him a wire trying to remind him of his wonderful wife and children), but he was too far gone. When he sang "Nancy With the Laughing Face" at a Copa opening, the audience turned to stare at Ava, sitting at a corner table, and then burst into hysterical laughter.

They were two stars trading magnitudes, the female rising on the fall of the male; and more, better, a share-cropper's daughter from North Carolina and a tough little monkey from the Jersey docks. How tough, everyone would see, and hear. Because Heifetz, Dorsey and Billie Holiday notwithstanding, nobody taught him more about singing than Ava Gardner did.

Each place I go each song I know the dream I dream each hopeless scheme the heartbreak only the lonely know ... Who could ever doubt that he knew how a loser felt? Violets for her furs, and blood. They could shoot to wound across ten thousand miles and never miss, and there was always somebody around to take a picture of it, until the outrages accumulated and took them both beyond reconciliation. Until, in the unforgettable update on the Orphic story, he turned around and changed her wonderful flesh and blood into a small golden totem that brought him up from the underworld faster than waking from a bad dream. That passage seemed to cure him of looking back. It was his toughest job, The Case of the Madonna and the Whore. He never cracked it, and he probably never closed the file. It almost killed him. After that, he became a very hard-boiled private dick indeed.

Refrain: *La ci darem la mano …*

In the myth, the young sailor on leave has twenty-four hours to find and win the one girl in the world who is meant only for him. If he finds her, he will be happy for the rest of his life. If not, he'll be alone, restless, half a man. The story traditionally expresses itself most fluently in technicolor musical-comedy, but it might play even better as a melodrama, the darker the better, in which it wouldn't matter by the end whether he finds her or not. In the collective dream sequence of the great career, the singing sailor became the kissing bandit became the pussy gangster. His cold deck was hot again, but was it full?

Spring Is Here

"I am a symmetrical man."

The story of his comeback is so familiar, at least to anybody over forty, that it's not worth retelling here. It has already entered the mainstream of American lore, a classic folktale of resurgence and undertow. Pope, chairman of the board, leader of the ratpack, *padrone*, master of the violent contradiction, watershed of fifty years of white American soul singing, the entertainers' entertainer. Very few people are really that attracted to the underdog. Everybody is hypnotized by a winner. If the winner is also a survivor, the triumph can be irresistible. And infectious.

Nobody had ever achieved that eminence in show business before, or since. It's hard to think of another public figure who has dared to appear so pregnant with his own history as Frank Sinatra did during the twenty years between Oscar night 1954 and his "retirement". For such a private man, and one who has been notorious almost as long as he's been famous, he was always remarkably free in exposing his secret self. His wild, suffering and even vicious self. So what do you want? Even if he told you everything, knowing isn't having; you wouldn't be satisfied. What's the problem, and what are you going to do about it?

◆

As he stepped from Governor Reagan's limousine on his way to a Republican fundraising, Maxine Cheshire of the Washington Post said, "Mr. Sinatra, do you think that your alleged association with the Mafia will prove to be the same embarrassment to Vice President Agnew that it was to the Kennedy Administration?"

"I don't worry about things like that," he answered, not unpleasantly. But when he saw her a few years later at a party, he called her a two-dollar cunt, stuck a couple of bills in her drink, and said, "Here, baby, that's what you're used to." Brutal, maybe, but a strong lesson to all journalists: never ask a man a question when you already know the answer.

◆

(*The House I Live In*, Take 3, b/w *It's a Long Way From Your House to My House*. The Kennedy Wing of his Palm Springs home, which Kennedy (probably) never used, was renamed the Spiro Agnew Wing. What politics would a winner embrace but the Politics of Winning? One was reminded of Robert Frost, who said that he was afraid of being too liberal when young for fear of becoming too conservative when old. A real danger not only for poets, but for puppets, paupers, pirates, pawns and kings. Especially kings.)

My Way

"We will never believe anything awful about Frank unless we hear him verify it." (From the Preamble to the Constitution of the Pittsburgh Society for Swooning Souls of the Sensational Sinatra, 1942)

"You try and subpoena me and you'll get a big fat fucking surprise."

He personally remembers what jewelry his friends and their wives like, and their clothing sizes. He has also forgotten or forgiven a lot of old slights, if not all. To call his generosity "legendary" is to imply that it doesn't exist, which is absurd, even libelous. Everybody knows of the time and the money that have gone to underprivileged children, to the sick and poor, to old showbiz friends in trouble (e.g., the blank check sent to George Raft during his troubles with the IRS, given in the understanding that it was good for up to a million dollars. How classy Raft must have felt — how classy he actually was — when he declined it. In this instance, what Sinatra gave was better than money, as he must have known.); the hours and the songs for oppressed minorities, for oppressive minorities, even to strangers. And not like Elvis Presley raining pathological Cadillacs on people, but anonymous, behind the screen, from the shadows. ("He has everything," his daughter once said, "he cannot sleep, he gives nice gifts, he is not happy, but he would not trade, even for happiness, what he is.")

And of course the songs themselves: Whether he was singing them for fifteen bucks a week or fifty grand a night, he only ever sang them one way, and we know which way that is.

("My Way", incidentally, is a song he claims to despise. It should really only be sung by men past sixty, and then not too often, and maybe not at all if the singer has a strong "September Song". Sinatra has the best.)

"That doesn't make them part of something. They said hello, you said hello. They came backstage. They thanked you. You offered them a drink. That was it. And it doesn't matter, anyway, does it? Most of the guys I knew, or met, are dead."

Frank Sinatra in song and story; the summing up, a distillation hot and salty as the tear that falls on the diamond in a pinky ring. The long haul, time in. And never mind what those cocksuckers say. They respect you, Frank.

The Song Is You

"When I sing I believe I'm honest."

Put your dreams away for another day and I will take their place in your heart … Consider the peculiar nature of a stardom lasting almost half a century, and the quality of the exchange between the stardom (not the star) and the audience. What makes you so sure that your opinion is really required?

Multivalent, incompatible, crying for a reconciliation of antagonistic parts: Wrathful/peaceful, artist/philistine, classy/vulgar, megastar and supercitizen, he kept everybody listening all those years for the unresolved chord whose solution could only be musical. Everyone who has ever been reached by the sound of his voice has a piece of the problem to weigh, and if you don't like who he slept with or ate with or stayed up late with, get rid of the sound. The next time it comes in, just refuse to recognize it.

◆

Solo spot for a baritone. From his spirit into yours, from his experience and isolation into ours. All by himself, no division between the singer and the song, incomparable, untouchable, singing the song of songs, the long slow ballad of money sex and power. A song from the source and the seat of the controversy, *Gee it's lonely really lonely at the top*, high teachings from the Voice, the story of a life sung softly with emotion to empty tables across the big room in the wee small hours of the Twentieth Century.

The Big Room. *1977*

Once, in a happy schoolboy mood, Siegel wrote a love poem for Virginia, scrawling it down laboriously with a pen, and gave it to her on her birthday. He put it into an envelope on which he had written "To My Sweetheart", and she later told Chick it made her cry. Long afterward, when she was talking to reporters in Florida about Ben Siegel, she said: "You know – he was never as tough as you guys made him – look at this lovely poem he wrote for me." She opened her purse and took it out, the paper now wrinkled and torn, and she started to read it aloud. Then, as though an unseen hand had touched her shoulder, she slowly folded it and put it away, and her eyes froze.
"Oh the hell with it," she said. "You bums wouldn't get it anyway."

— *We Only Kill Each Other*, Dean Jennings

Bartenders Union showed thanks and esteem to Frank Sinatra closing night at Caesar's Palace with a special bar stool, plus a lifetime gold union card. A smaller stool was also brought onstage by Local 165 boss Jack Stafford for Dean Martin, who never showed up. Quote Sinatra about the gift, "I think it's one of the most important awards in the world because I'm a saloon singer."

— Bill Willard in *Variety*, 3/23/83

If you could get up above the city tonight and oversee the action the way they monitor the casinos, moving over catwalks, looking down through peepholes and two-way mirrors or just sitting in the office watching it on closed-circuit, you'd have it over them for once, watching them for a change, and you'd see the wheel that holds all the smaller wheels that seem so enormous when it's your money or your fantasy that's riding on it, and you wouldn't need a computer or even a pencil to figure the odds, or see who really has the juice around here. High up with your eye-in-the-sky, the years would evaporate in a way that the architects of this timeless place never dreamed possible, and it would all go by for you again: The Paiute, the first Army scout, the Mormons, the 49ers, the railroad/highway/dam/hotel/career builders, the Bug and his boys and the millions who saw it his way, the big draws and the drawn, while Frémont Trace, Arrowhead Trail, Union Pacific, Highway 91 and The Strip lapse into one another in sequence. From this elevation, you wouldn't have to stop there.

The city is sinking fast, six feet in forty years, mostly from water depletion, the action of foundation seeking bedrock, helped immeasurably by shockwaves from the nuclear testing grounds a hundred miles away. It's sinking in our minds too, maybe even faster, like an old fascination that's merely interesting now. Cost-distance is a lot of it. There's not so much loose change now, putting gas in your tank isn't what it used to be, and unless you have your own plane, it's a drag flying anywhere. There's Atlantic City back east, and anyway, the permissions that were so peculiar to the place have been issued almost everywhere by now, public vice and private virtue. The shadow stakes of high risk have jumped to Miami; it's Florida's time to learn how quickly easy money can turn a state. And the golden shills aren't pulling them in anymore either. You can run a cable into your house for less than it costs you to spend an evening in Vegas, and they'll all come in and play for you there; a bargain, of a kind. Everything we ever meant by Las Vegas will just be another old story, maybe our children will want to hear about it some day; live acts, buzz and hush, standing ovations, big rooms. The emblazoning process of the old show business is already a convention of past time, a figure in a book of spent hours that nobody reads anymore. Las Vegas Ha Muriendo, Viva Las Vegas.

Maybe some mad billionaire will take it over, restore and preserve it like Williamsburg, turn it into a Prosperity Museum. Maybe alkali, the old leveller, will make its big comeback, and it will be alkali, not silver and gold, juice, talent, guns or a fantastic body that will be the last currency here. You'll drive through and stop along the road, listen for the old hum and hear nothing but the sand, eroding, erasing, forming, re-forming and erasing some more forever... *You've been wonderful ladies and gentlemen, kiss kiss, God bless*... then gone. And once they've gone and we let them go, they don't come back. Don't say it hasn't been fun. Let's have a great big hand for the sand...